THE AUCTORATI

by Jarrod D. King

The Auctorati

ISBN-13: 978-0-9981187-3-4

To *family*

This story takes place six years before the events in
Pangaea: Unsettled Land.

CHAPTER ONE

L ibra thought he had defeated all of the henchmen, but the barrel of a BAC rifle pressed against his spine was proof he was wrong. He was scared; however, he didn't look back—choosing instead to listen to the nonchalant male voice calling from behind.

"You wouldn't want to do that."

Libra let the coarse threads of rope slip from his fingers and stood up slowly, arms raised. He was surprised. He didn't expect the man who'd hired these thugs to make an appearance. "You won't get away with this, Talon."

Libra kept his eyes on the woman in front of him. Her hair was dark, as were her eyes and lips. His recon mission to find out what Talon was up to had been halted when he saw she was a hostage. Despite his efforts to untie her, the rope was still taut around her wrists. The day was breaking, and an amber light shone through the broken windows of the old building. The rising sun was hot on his face, which was covered from the nose down by a solid black bandana.

"Oh...I think I will, Auctorat." Talon nodded to the woman. "This one tried to strike when I was least expecting, but I'm always expecting." Mid-sentence, six more people with swords and BACs came through the front entrance and surrounded them. "Now go!"

Libra turned, his brow skewed in confusion. The crew of mercenaries surrounding him, known as the XN, lifted their weapons as a warning. "I didn't take you for a coward," Libra said to Talon. Grasping at the shards of his mission, he stalled as much as could to get any information out of Talon. "Too afraid to fight me?" He watched the man with black cornrowed hair lower his left hand, which was holding the gun. Talon was brown-skinned, but the shadow under which he stood made him appear darker. He wore a cape twisted to cover his right arm.

2

Talon sighed and laughed. "What a ridiculous statement. Never. I wouldn't hesitate to kill you if I saw the use, but there is none. I ought to, as much trouble as you've caused, but—"

"You don't want blood on your hands when you get caught. That's too bad, 'cause you're covered."

Talon grinned. "Prove it."

A shot rang through building and one of the henchmen fell over. Talon whipped his head back and saw the same thing as Libra. One of the hooded men had turned on the others. The turncoat had used his sword to take down another. Libra took advantage of the confusion and drew his sword to end things with Talon once and for all.

He swung but was shocked to see Talon had blocked using nothing but his right arm! It wasn't severed or scarred, but it felt like a clang against metal. The strike left a horizontal split in the cape and it fell to reveal a metallic prosthetic from the shoulder down. The fingernails at its end extended into claws.

Talon frowned and pushed Libra back. "You owe me a cape."

Pandemonium ensued. The traitorous henchman continued to fight the others while Libra attacked vital spots. Talon blocked each move, never needing to draw a sword, using only his metal arm to do so.

Libra grew frustrated as each of his strikes were blocked. Then, Talon went on the offensive, pushing Libra back until he lost his balance. He almost ended it with a swing of his huge claw, but Libra dodged back into a beam.

Libra could hear the whistle of Talon's claws pass his face as he dodged again. This time, the strike shattered the beam behind him. Libra fell to the floor where the hostage last sat, but he noticed she was gone. Only the rope that once bound her wrists remained. In that moment, he noticed something strange. The rope had been burned through.

He started to hear cracking noises coming from above and turned his attention to the ceiling. It was about to cave in.

Talon backed off. "We'll meet again, I'm sure, Auctorat."

Cement and dirt from the ceiling collapsed in between them. Libra rolled back to dodge the debris. When he looked back, Talon was gone.

"Dammit," said a voice. "That was my one shot." It was the turncoat. He removed his hood, revealing his young brown face with hair that'd had enough heat applied to turn coarse curly hair straight. His brown eyes were full of disappointment. He put a hand on his hip and shook his head. "The Auctorat just had to be here. Look at us now."

"Who are you?" Libra called out.

The man hopped up and over the debris to lend Libra a hand. Once he grabbed hold, he lifted him up and said, "The name's Micks. Charmed. And yours?"

Libra mocked a laugh and just shook his head.

"What? Don't I get something for helping out the Auctorat?"

"Helped out? All this chaos?"

"Would you rather be dead? The first thing I saw was Talon holding a BAC to your back."

"He wouldn't have killed me—"

"And how do you know his little soldiers wouldn't?"

Libra hesitated, but knew he was right. "I'm sorry. Thank you, but I can't give you my identity."

"Fair enough. I assume you were here for the same thing as him? The Dragon's Bit?"

"The Dragon's Bit? What is that? I'm just trying to find out what Talon is up to."

"So, you don't know? To think I have something on the Auctorat! The Dragon's Bit is precisely what Talon is up to. He's looking for it. That's why the city's been so quiet lately. He must have a lead."

"What is it?"

"It's exactly what it sounds like. A bit for a dragon. Kind of like for a horse, just...bigger. Supposedly, it's an artifact of the old stories where the fire spirit inhabited a man. Their rapport was so good, the spirit granted its host this artifact that allowed him to take control of a dragon."

Hunting for a fantastic legend seemed like a stretch, even for Talon. Dragons only roamed far off to the west and they were untamable. "And that's supposed to be real?"

Micks shrugged. "Supposed to be. Nobody's ever seen it. If it were real, could you imagine?"

"Talon with a dragon? We'd have to call it quits." Libra began looking around for a clue as to why Talon's search for the artifact had brought him here.

"My guess would be this," Micks said. He reached down into the rubble and pulled out a small brown book. He grinned at Libra's look of confusion. "You were thinking 'why here?', right? He's been looking for these."

"I thought he was looking for a bit."

"He is, but these are guides to the location of the Dragon's Bit. Talon seems like he'd do anything for these."

Libra reached out a hand. "I need that."

"Not so fast. I have my reasons for holding onto this one, but there's one more."

"Where?"

Micks shrugged. "Not sure. You'll have to keep tabs on Talon for that. I've just attacked the people who were my only *in* to his circle. I'm out of the group now."

"How do you know all of this?"

"Now, is it really fair to keep asking me questions? You've barely told me anything about yourself. Come on, maybe we could help each other out."

Libra rolled his eyes and walked away toward the front door, away from the scene. There was no way he was giving up his identity. It was his safety— his way of protecting his normal life from the crazy one of chasing down criminals. But it had been a good day, after all. Now that he knew what Talon was after, he figured it shouldn't be that hard to find. He'd find the book on his own and use it as a bargaining chip with Talon and force him to publicly resign in exchange. Micks had a point. The way Talon made a personal appearance with his goons was out of character. He seemed to want the books more than anything. Libra knew it would work. He'd push Talon out of power once and for all.

CHAPTER TWO

Micks knew coming away from that fight empty-handed wouldn't feel good. So, he was happy when he'd found a strange book amongst the rubble. When he had picked it up, he thought it odd the wood around it was in embers. None of its pages were burned, however. It was almost as if it was the source of the burning. Regardless, his mission was to kill Talon, but maybe bringing his client what Talon was after would suffice.

He saw a long wheeler parked down the block with tinted windows and knew it was waiting for him. As he walked toward the vehicle, he swallowed, thinking about what explanation he would have to come up with for his failure. Micks needed this money. This was supposed to be his last job. Then, he'd have enough money to move to Reor, live well, and start fresh. He needed to get out of this god-forsaken city, but failing wasn't the way. The Auctorat was really to blame. If only he hadn't been there, nobody would've been on guard and the double-cross could have been clean and easy. But he was there, and he couldn't just watch the city's hero die, could he? All that time schmoozing, learning about Talon's plan, and working his way into the XN had gone up in smoke.

The door to the wheeler opened, beckoning him to enter.

"Micks. How'd it go?" said the voice inside.

Micks took his seat on the opposite side and felt the purr of the engine as the vehicle rolled away. The man across from him was well-dressed, had a full head of blonde hair, a square jaw, and a large blonde mustache. Micks took note of his earnest expression. "You don't waste any time."

"Time is money. Tell me. Did you get him?"

Micks took a deep breath and stared briefly at the floor.

"Dammit. I don't like that look. So, he got away?"

"Yeah," said Micks. He felt around the seat for the book and held it in his hand. "But, I found—"

"Un-be-lieveable! You know, when I hired you, my gut told me you were too much of a…dandy to do what needed to be done. Too soft."

Micks recoiled at the insult. "Don't do that. I got in this close," he gestured with his fingers. "I had him. But the Auctorat showed up."

"I don't give a shit if Elao himself showed up. I'm paying you to do a job, son! Talon's ruining my business. Nobody realizes, but he's the one responsible for the state of the city—not the mayor. And, that tax on crystals he got him to pass has people running from my company to the next town over to buy from his company."

Micks knew this already. In addition to hearing it plenty of times from Mr. Draw, it was his job to find out all the dirt on his target. He at least did that part. "Speaking of payment—"

"No. I only pay for a job well done. Maybe you're not the right guy."

This couldn't seriously be happening. This last job was his ticket out. If he couldn't do it, all of his dreams would go up in smoke. "I can do it. I can do it! Just give me another chance, I promise you. What can I do now? Just tell me."

Mr. Draw sighed and pinched the bridge of his nose. "The mayor."

"What? You, yourself, just said he wasn't involved—"

"Not knowingly—at first. But the kid signed the bill. He's not as naive as he pretends. He's involved now and needs to go just like Talon. I wouldn't be surprised if he's taking a cut of the profits by now."

Micks bit his tongue. He wasn't going to argue. If the mayor needed to die, he needed to die. Life-changing money was on the line. "So, the mayor."

"And a bonus if you can get Talon at the same time."

The wheels in Micks' head began to turn. Strategizing was his favorite part. If he could just get them in the same room together... "Got it."

The wheeler pulled to a stop by a small canal that ran through the edge of town. He opened the door, got out, and heard Mr. Draw's last remark before closing it behind him: "Make sure you do."

CHAPTER THREE

The dirty ground of the back alley was Kandyce's only comfort, and it wasn't much. She sat there with her back against the wall as the sun periodically made a visit in between the stone buildings. There was a heaviness in her. There was always a heaviness in her, but failing to kill Talon once again made it impossible to ignore. She hated this world. And the world hated her, because she was an Etherean...a magic user. If only she could get her revenge against Talon, maybe she'd find a way to live with herself.

Fucking Talon, she thought. *Damn Auctorat.* If the *hero* hadn't shown up, she would've been able to take Talon down with the element of surprise.

Without destroying the place, even. The Auctorat came in and gave Talon time for his mercenaries to show up.

She reached in her pocket and pulled out a ring with a small crystal which glowed red. She thought of Mira. Mira had given this to her just days before she was murdered in the street by the XN. God, she missed her. Mira used to make everything tolerable, but now Kandyce couldn't just go on with her life knowing Mira's killers were out there.

These crystals were expensive. They were extremely valuable to Ethereans because they were a way to store ether—magic power—as a backup. With one, Kandyce could use fire when there was no fire around. The large crystal Kandyce wanted had been way out of her price range, so Mira surprised her with a ring. Kandyce would always remember that moment: Mira arriving home at night—the dim, amber light of the room illuminating her equally amber skin and long, dark hair. Kandyce had been tired and was close to sleep, but Mira climbed in bed next to her and held her close. She felt her hand being pulled up and the cold metal band of the ring sliding down her finger. Kandyce pulled her hand back to see the jewel and felt her heart would burst.

"Where did you get this?" Kandyce had asked.

"Never mind that, my love," Mira responded, in her usual soft, wispy voice. "Just know that I'm holding up my end of the deal. You promised to always protect me, but I want to protect you, too. I'm no fighter like you, but this is my way."

Kandyce turned in bed to face her. A moment of silence passed as they looked into each others' eyes. Then, Kandyce said, "I love you." She pulled Mira closer to her and pressed their lips together. It was a moment Kandyce wished could have lasted forever.

The sweetness of that memory always ended in a pang of frustration, perhaps even rage. Now, in the alley, Kandyce slid the ring on her finger and placed her head in her hands. She hadn't cried much since she was a child. It was even hard for her now, but she somehow managed a tear from each eye. It wasn't a full release like she wanted, but it would have to do for now. She wiped her eyes, stood up, and inhaled a deep breath.

Now what, she asked herself. She didn't know where to find Talon. Even if she did, she knew she wouldn't have the chance she'd had a moment ago. Her only option, it seemed, was to find the Auctorat.

CHAPTER FOUR

L ibra was frustrated during his walk back home. He'd removed his bandana before anyone saw him. And since he left his fight with Talon, he couldn't help but feel like he was no closer to his goal. He wanted nothing more than to see his hometown achieve its former glory, but when its mayor went rogue, the whole place went to shit. Libra remembered seeing Talon standing next to the mayor on camera once with a smug expression and superior posture. He knew then Probuston was in for some hard times. Soon after, the crime rate skyrocketed, and the mayor turned a blind eye to most of it. Even then, Libra thought something would turn it around. Surely someone would stand up. It didn't happen. The rich folks moved away, the neighborhoods stopped getting the care they needed, and almost every day there came word of a murder or robbery.

As Libra opened the door to his home, he heard a cough. It was his mother. He had long ago decided to live at her house to take care of her. While many would think it a failure for a twenty-six-year-old man to live with his mother, her failing health had made his decision easy. She was in her usual spot on the couch in the living room. She lifted her head from the arm of the couch and looked at him with inquisitive eyes. "Where have you been?"

He shrugged, trying to act natural. "Just out for a walk."

"Did you fall or something?"

His clothes were still dusty from the debris. He'd been too introspective to even remember to dust himself off.

He gave a nervous laugh, "Yeah. How are you feeling?" he asked, switching the subject to avoid any further discussion of his whereabouts.

His mother shrugged. "As good as I can be, I guess. I miss our walks, Libra"

"Me too, Mom. Remember our playground?"

She smiled. "How could I forget? You used to run all over the place when you were little. The slides, the swings, the geysers…"

"Don't forget the monkey bars," Libra laughed.

"Oh, of course not. You were so proud the first time you made it all the way across without falling. And then you grew up on me."

"Well, we still enjoyed it from afar. Part of our walks through the park. Until…" Libra didn't want to finish the sentence. He could tell his mother already had in her head.

Libra remembered when it all changed. One day, after a week of absence, Libra had returned home for a visit, and their usual lively walk through the park was dampened at the sight of destruction. The slides were spray-painted in vulgarities, the geyser didn't work, and two of three swings were missing while the last hung on one chain. He remembered that moment because he saw his mother stop and wince at the sight. She wanted to go home, much earlier this time than any other time. Their walks died in that moment and whenever Libra visited his mother, she wanted to stay seated in the house. After a while, her health declined to the point where simply getting up was a struggle. That's when Libra had decided enough was enough. He wasn't naive enough to believe that a decimated playground was enough to sicken his mother, but it'd played its part.

"I'm going to run up," he said instead. Everything around him seemed to be dying. He couldn't stand to see it. "I need to take a shower."

His mother nodded. "Okay."

And it was all because of the mayor and Talon's corruption.

Having been a part of the city's police force, the Enforcers, had given Libra insight into where crime was usually taking place. But the Enforcers were ineffective. How could they enforce the laws of a corrupt system? Libra broke ties with the group but kept his black bandana, something all Enforcers tied around their arms as a sign of authority. Instead, he wrapped it over his nose and mouth to conceal his identity and went out to stop the crimes that had torn apart the city.

Almost every crime he stopped led back to Talon in some way. And to have been in a fight with him and lose, it was humiliating. Talon was strong, and that metal claw had been a surprise. Who knew what other surprises he had in store?

Libra traveled up the carpeted stairs to his room. If he was going to make a change in the city, he needed to change up his strategy. Forcing Talon's resignation was still the plan, but if a fight ever broke out, he needed to be ready. Talon had a team. Why not him? And if he was going to team up with someone, the question was: who?

Despite the carpet in the hallway, the floorboards creaked with each step. It was a wonder he ever got out of the house unheard. He opened the door to his room, removed his black jacket and jeans, and sat on the bed. His room was a mess. Clothes were thrown haphazardly on every surface he could see. His bed was unmade and a scattered pile of papers almost seemed to float in midair as they sat atop small items and every inch of his desk. He shifted his attention to the newspaper clipping he posted on the wall. It was the only other thing posted up beside a photo of his celebrity crush, Princess Annonym. The headline read, 'CRIMINALS BEWARE THE AUCTORAT OF PROBUSTON' with a picture of a masked Libra fighting underneath. It always gave Libra a boost of pride in what he was doing, to see some of the citizens were grateful to his protest. But right now, he felt pretty powerless. If he couldn't bring Talon down, what was the point of it all?

He thought back to the guy he met at the warehouse moments ago. *Maybe we could help each other out*, he'd said. Libra had refused to divulge any information about himself, but some help would be nice. Micks was a little too nosey for Libra's liking, so he wouldn't be going back to him. However, he did know of someone he could bring in for help.

CHAPTER FIVE

The night was mild. Almost too warm for the bandana around Libra's face. As he stepped down the moonlit street, he kept sticking his finger behind the piece of fabric to wipe off small annoying beads of sweat. After a while, he could hear that he was close to his target—the man he wanted to recruit. The sound of spray paint against the wall of the building around the corner was unmistakable. When Libra was an Enforcer, he'd seen this guy's moves. He was a good fighter and Libra remembered his attitude towards Talon. With so many henchmen around Talon, Libra knew he couldn't take him alone. He'd need some backup, and this was the guy.

Libra turned the corner and watched him put the finishing touches on another piece of what he called art. It was a quote written in calligraphy. Libra thought it was actually quite nice. It read:

'Down with Mayor Wilhelm and his parrot.' — V

Libra decided to get him before he stopped. "Hey. Vinzant!"

The vandal's head jerked to face who called out to him. He smiled and stood up from his crouched position. "Really? The Auctorat? As if the Enforcers weren't enough. Don't you have something better to do, like bust up a gang or something?" He chuckled. "All this time I thought we were on the same side." He threw his spray can into the cloth satchel he had on his back. It was strapped diagonally in the front from shoulder to hip and acted as a holster for his sword. He did it all while keeping a close eye on Libra.

Libra could sense Vinzant was on edge. He tried to stop Vinzant as he began to step away. "I just need a moment."

"Sorry, fresh out," said Vinzant as he dashed around the opposite corner of the building.

Libra mumbled curse words and ran after him. "Wait!" As he turned the corner, he caught sight of Vinzant running down the street. He tried to catch up and heard Vinzant taunting him.

"Give it up, Auctorat. Even the cops have a hard time tailing me." He disappeared around another dark corner.

Vinzant was fast, agile, a skilled swordsman and marksman, and was already familiar with working in the shadows—the best choice for a partner Libra could hope for. It was the only reason Libra decided to chase him down. He just hated that all of Vinzant's strong points were working against him right now.

Libra caught up and made a slow turn into the corner while drawing his sword. He was wary of an ambush and heard footsteps. He cocked his head. They weren't coming from in front of him, but above him. He looked up to see Vinzant shimmying up the center of the narrow alley with each foot hopping between the walls. Left, right, left, right.

What in the…? Libra spied a drain to his left and used it to climb after him. When he reached the rooftop, he fell over at the sound of a loud pop. He froze, unsure if he had been hit, but felt no pain.

"That was a warning shot," said Vinzant as he lowered his BAC.

Libra watched as he turned and jumped over to the next rooftop. "God! Just wait a minute!" he yelled. He picked himself up to follow.

After jumping from one roof to another, dodging chimneys and patio furniture, Vinzant slowed to a stop. There was too wide a distance between where he stood and the next building. All that was below was traffic and people milling about. They'd run into a busier part of town.

Libra caught up and keeled over, bracing his hands on his knees. "You're pretty fast," he wheezed.

Vinzant turned, pulling his blade from the sheath at his back. "I told you to leave me alone. You know, even nice guys like me can turn when backed into a corner." He ran full speed toward Libra.

Libra stuck out the palm of his hand and pleaded, "Wait, wait!" He had to think fast and draw his sword to block Vinzant's strike.

Vinzant's voice rang out over the sound of crashing swords. His voice punctuated each strike as he wore Libra down. "I really hate to...do this to you, buddy, but...I don't have time for a jail cell."

Libra stumbled back with each swing and felt fear creeping into his system. If he didn't do something now, this man was going to kill him. "Calm down! I'm not after–" but he could see Vinzant wasn't listening. "Vinzant!"

"You tired, dude?" Vinzant taunted. With his last swing, he continued, "Hows about you go to sleep!"

Libra gritted his teeth and mustered up all of his strength to deflect Vinzant's strike with a spin. He rammed into his open guard with his shoulder and knocked Vinzant back—far enough for Vinzant to lose control of his footing. He tripped and went screaming over the edge of the building. Libra dropped his sword and ran to the edge just in time to catch Vinzant's foot.

As Vinzant hung upside down, he calmed himself. He gave a nervous chuckle and a whistle while lifting his thumb. "Nice catch!"

"I just want to talk."

"Dude, I'm sold. Just don't let me fall."

***

Libra and Vinzant stood at the edge of the rooftop overlooking the life of the streets below: people going into bars alone and leaving hand in hand with someone else. Wheelers roared through the streets adding to the white noise of the city. All of it was drowned out to Vinzant by the question that was just posed to him.

"You want to team up...with me?" Vinzant shook his head in disbelief. "Are you serious?"

"Yeah. What do you say? Enough tagging. You can actually do something for the city. Like I said, if we can find this Dragon's Bit book before Talon, we have some power. We'll force him and the mayor to publicly resign before giving it to him –"

"Or not…"

"…and we can take down Talon together. Finally get this city back to the way it was. I don't expect him to take that suggestion without a fight, though. That's why I need you."

Vinzant's deep blue eyes revealed a joy at the prospect, but he was still a little skeptical. "Before I say 'okay', I have to trust you."

Libra hadn't expected him to say yes so easily, not after that fight. "Okay. What do you need?"

"Take off the mask."

Libra exhaled and turned. He wasn't comfortable with anyone knowing his identity, but what choice did he have? He reached behind his head and untied the bandana.

Vinzant's expression morphed from shock to amusement. He laughed, "Oh my God! The Auctorat's a freakin' cop!"

"You recognize me?"

"Of course, I do. You took me in a few times, you jerk."

"I left the Enforcers a while ago to do this. They're a part of the government, so their hands are tied. If we team up, we have a chance at really changing something. Can we let bygones be bygones?"

Vinzant shrugged. "Yeah, sure. Count me in. I'd love to give the mayor's mansion a new paint job, too." They sealed their commitment with a handshake and Vinzant asked, "So, what's next?"

"One of the Enforcers gets information about illegal activity they can't pursue. Or they could, but they turn a blind eye to it on orders from the mayor. She gives me the info, so I can take care of it."

"Sounds like not all of them are just falling in line. Good."

"So, we talk to her, see what's happening, and get what Talon wants before he does."

"Sounds like a plan."

CHAPTER SIX

Probuston was no Reor, but Talon had always sensed the possibilities lying beneath. Mayor Wilhelm was naïve, a man-child who had simply been given his position from the influence of his late father. Talon's influence was one of his strong suits. And now the mayor was alone, it was a muscle he used every day.

The day was bright and clear, and Talon enjoyed the warmth of the sun on his face as he sat on the large balcony of the mayor's estate. He'd decided today would be a fine day and took the first sip of his tea. Delicious.

"Good morning, Talon."

Talon turned from facing the cityscape of Probuston to see Wilhelm. "Wil! Good morning."

"Enjoying the day, I see," he said, as he took a spot next to Talon.

"It's not every day you have a moment to yourself. You must enjoy it while you can."

"No truer statement has been uttered, my man. Are you having tea?" He signaled the butler waiting next to the door for a cup of his own.

Talon noticed a pensive expression on Wilhelm's face. "Is something the matter?"

"I've been thinking."

Talon knew that wasn't a good sign. Wilhelm, at the tender age of thirty-two, thought he knew all there was to being a great leader. He knew nothing, but Talon didn't have the station to tell him what to do outright. So, whenever Wilhelm thought, Talon had to work harder to guide his mind where it needed to go. He folded the book he was reading and laid it on the table, readying himself for the boy's nonsense. "I'm listening."

"I think we should lift the crystal tax."

"Absolutely not." Ever since he'd been able to get Wilhelm to sign it into law, his business's profits had gone up. He couldn't possibly roll it back now.

"Well, just listen a minute." The butler returned with his tea, but Wilhelm continued. "We got the funding we needed for the university, but at what cost? The city hasn't gotten any better because of it. In fact, people are spending their money outside of the city now where crystals are cheaper."

"You really care what the Ethereans are doing?"

"When it impacts us as a whole, yes. The whole point was to place the pain of this tax where it hurt less. That was on the Ethereans. Who knew how bad it would get for us? Stores are closing up and people are moving out."

"Ethereans are moving out," he corrected. "I'm surprised at you. Many would think that a good thing. Wilhelm, stay the course. Once the university gets into full swing, the city will get back to how it was. Remember what I said? That I—"

"Yeah, yeah, you were the one who basically ended the war."

"That's right. The general made the final call, but I was the Queen's advisor. I got her ready. I know what I'm doing."

"Then why are you here, Talon? Why aren't you still back in the Middle Third sitting pretty next to the queen?"

"Like you, she was too young for her position. Even more so, she was only twelve. Ending the war, being responsible for the lives lost...it changed her. Queen Aeothesca finally understood her power as a ruler, but still couldn't face what she'd done. So, she fired me, her sole advisor, and replaced me with a whole team of advisors."

"She felt manipulated. I can relate."

Talon lifted the book from the table and pretended to read again. "If that is what you truly think of me, then I suppose you made your decision."

Wilhelm sighed. "I want you on board, Talon. I don't know if I could do this without you."

"I don't know, either. Which is why you should listen—" He stopped himself and took a breath. "Sleep on it. Don't make a decision today. You'll know what's right." *Because I'll tell you*, he thought.

Wilhelm nodded and took a sip of his tea. "Yeah, I'll do that."

Talon continued to look at the words in front of him in mock fashion while waiting for Wilhelm to take his leave. Once he did, Talon reached into his pocket and pulled out a small comm. He flicked it on, dialed a number, and stood up to walk over to the balcony rail while waiting for an answer. He saw the butler out of the corner of his eye and made a waving gesture. "Leave."

The person on the other end picked up. "Tal?"

"Hello, brother."

"What is it, Tal? I'm busy."

"I think I'm losing him."

"Wilhelm? You better not. Business in that area has been booming ever since you got him to sign that tax into law. I can't lose that territory. It's one of my biggest earners."

"I don't know if I can stop him this time."

"Failure's not an option. Tal, what are you calling me for with this?"

"Can you cut him in?"

"To the business?"

"He'll be more likely to keep the tax in place if he's getting something out of it," Talon said.

"And risk finding out about this? About you? Think about it. Even if he doesn't completely banish you and destroy my business, he'll start demanding more and more. And pretty soon, you'll be his bitch. Is that what you want? A repeat of the Middle Third?" Talon said nothing, waiting for this little tirade to end. "You know what the difference between you and him is? You and me even? I own my business. He's the mayor. We're bosses. When are you gonna finally get on that level? Boss up!"

Talon scowled at the command from his brother. He fixed his lips to quip back but thought better of it. Instead, he said, "Our."

"What?"

"Our business. You keep saying your business, but last I checked, I own part of it."

He could hear his brother chuckle on the other end. "Sure, Tal. Our business." The sound of a click signaled his brother's departure from the conversation.

Talon hated his patronizing tone. And what he hated even more was that somewhere inside, he felt he was right. For too long, he'd played in other people's shadows. That needed to change. Getting rich was one thing, but power was what he needed—especially if he was ever going to get revenge against the Queen. He was already working on it. He'd waited decades. It was only a matter of time now...

CHAPTER SEVEN

"Apparently, there's a big heist planned at the Grand Library," said the Enforcer.

Libra stood across from her in the back alley of the Enforcer's station with Vinzant just out of earshot. She leaned against the brick wall behind her. She had short black hair that perfectly cupped the roundness of her brown face. She continued, "Talon's ordered the place seized and searched, unofficially, of course."

"Meaning illegally," said Libra. "And he's using the XN to do it, I bet."

"Any idea what they're looking for?"

"I have an idea."

"And?"

"It's best if you stay in the dark for now. Seems like anyone who knows is in deeper trouble."

"Mysterious. Well, sorry I can't help anymore."

"You've done plenty. Thanks."

She pushed herself from the wall and re-entered the building saying, "Go get 'em, Auctorat."

Now that Libra knew Talon's next target, his mind entered a tunnel as he walked on. Thoughts swirled in his head: *Do I have enough time before they show up? That has to be where the second book is hidden.* He barely heard the knock of his black boots against the old brick walkway. Nor did he notice Vinzant following close behind until he broke his concentration.

"What did she say?"

"The Grand Library."

"The second clue?"

"Yeah."

"Gee, you're cheery," said Vinzant.

Libra sensed Vinzant falling behind and looked over his to shoulder to see him peering into the darkness further back. "What's up?"

"...Nothing," he said. And they moved on.

***

Kandyce caught her breath and tried to control her nerves. This was all for Mira. She had to be at her best. She stood perpendicular to the brick wall at the corner—head, shoulders, and back completely against it. She'd finally found the Auctorat, but had almost been caught. With one last deep breath, Kandyce settled in her mind to be extra careful. If the Auctorat was onto something, she knew Talon wouldn't be too far behind.

***

From the rooftop of an open plaza, Libra peered down onto the Grand Library. Spotlights brightened the building's beige stone columns, giving it the look of a safe haven in the night. He knew it was anything but. The various shops were closed at this time of night and hardly any wheelers drove past in the street.

Vinzant stood next to him, arms crossed. "You ready, buddy?"

"Yeah. Looks like they haven't shown up yet. Maybe we can get what they're after for ourselves before they get here."

Vinzant whined, "Aw, I was in the mood for cracking skulls."

Libra chuckled and started climbing down the ladder in front of them. "There will be time for that soon enough, young protégé. You might even get your own skull cracked."

Vinzant followed. "Protégé? Who do you think's running the show here?"

Once they reached the ground, they dodged pools of light from lamps lining the center walkway and stepped through the shadows. The path led to a street crossing lined by hedges. Just as they approached, the headlights of a wheeler came rolling down. Libra had to pull Vinzant by the arm to stop him from vaulting over. They ducked behind the small shrubs until the vehicle passed, and then they jumped over. After a sprint to the other side of the street, they hit another obstacle. The lights illuminating the library were bright enough to make almost anything visible within its radius.

Vinzant said, "Looks like we'll be on camera, Auctorat. Ready for your close-up?"

Libra surveyed the scene a little more and eyed one of the spotlights on the corner of the building. "If only we could turn that one off, it would be our shortest path." Vinzant raised his BAC for a shot, but Libra swatted it away. "No! That's too loud."

"Well, I don't have a slingshot, so unless you have a better idea—"

"I can help," said a voice.

Both turned swiftly on their heels. Libra drew his sword and Vinzant pointed his gun, both unsure where the voice had come from. Libra noticed a figure walking towards them from the curb with her hands raised.

"I don't mean any harm," she said. "I just want Talon as much as you do."

Libra looked her up and down until a memory clicked. "You…you were the girl at the abandoned building."

"Nice to see you again, Auctorat."

The two men lowered their weapons. "You followed us?" Libra asked.

"Like I said, I'm not after you. I'm after Talon. I knew you'd lead me to him. If I was after you, you'd be dead by now."

Vinzant raised his eyebrows and looked at Libra. "Uh-oh! Fightin' words."

Libra said, "I'm pretty sure I could handle my—" His words were cut short at the sight of what the woman pulled out of her pocket. It was a small ring, but the stone was made of crystal, and it glowed red. Libra stared at the ring and then back at her, surprised at the realization she was an Etherean.

"Yeah," she said. "That a problem for you?"

Libra shook his head, "No, but you got a way of taking out that light?"

She walked a few steps past them and raised her hand with the ring. Libra's heart skipped a beat when her hand was suddenly engulfed in flame. The fire ceased from spreading and she collected it in her palm until it formed a small concentrated spike. Almost like a dagger. She concentrated on the spotlight and the flame shot out of her hand and onto the light. With a flick of her wrist, she made sure the fire didn't go wild once it hit. Then, she struggled to squeeze her hand closed as the light popped, snuffing out the flame. A trail of shadow appeared in its wake.

Vinzant whistled. "Not bad."

Libra regarded his new magical ally with the same sentiment. "Thanks," he started, not quite sure how to finish. "...You got a name?"

"Kandyce. Do you?"

Libra laughed, as if he would fall for that. "The Auctorat."

Libra started down the path and the others followed. They got to the edge of the building and found a large window on the wall a few feet above their heads. Libra said, "This is you, Vinzant."

Vinzant jumped high enough for his fingertips to grasp the very edge of the window. He looked catlike as the bottom of his feet clung to the wall. He reached behind him to pull out his sword. Libra saw him holding on with one hand and couldn't believe his strength. Vinzant used the hilt of the sword to break through the glass. "Be right down," he said, pulling himself up and in.

Libra waited in an awkward silence with Kandyce. He broke it with, "So, what's your beef with Talon?"

"He killed my girlfriend."

Libra winced. "He did? I'm so sorry."

"Well, not him in particular, but his little gang… And thanks."

Libra could sense there was more to the story but decided not to pry. "We're gonna bring him down soon, so you don't have to worry."

Kandyce laughed, "Nice try. You're not getting rid of me here. You weren't able to kill him last time. Even if he doesn't show up tonight, all of his thugs are going back in a body bag."

The metal door creaked open and Vinzant peeked out from inside. "Right this way, ladies and gentlemen."

Kandyce rolled her eyes and asked Libra, "Who is this guy, anyway?"

Libra playfully shrugged and walked in.

"You never heard of V? Street artist, extraordinaire?" Vinzant said.

"Nope."

"Well, you will when I save the city from Talon."

"Since when does the sidekick do the saving?"

"Sidekick?!" Vinzant said, reeling back.

"Guys," Libra interrupted. "Any idea where to find this clue?"

Vinzant shrugged, "We're just following your lead, big guy."

Kandyce smiled, unable to help herself. "Like I said. Sidekick."

"The last clue was a small book with a really ornate cover," said Libra.

"What is this about a book?" asked Kandyce.

"It's what Talon's after. It's a clue to the whereabouts of a magical artifact: The Dragon's Bit."

"And what does this Dragon's Bit do?"

"I don't know. I didn't get a good look at the first clue. Somebody else got to it first."

"The double agent?"

"Right. So, I don't know what it does, but if it's important enough for Talon to go through all this trouble, then we can't let him have it."

"I see. Well, it sounds like a rare book. And this place must have a section for them."

The inside of the Grand Library was wide and deep with row after row of ceiling-high shelves, fully-stocked with books. The dim lighting bounced off of the wood floor and furniture, just enough for them to make their way through. They passed by small tables with chairs, a few couches, and computer stations until they reached the big circular desk in the middle. Nobody was working, of course, so finding the section they were looking for would be something they had to do on their own.

"There's a map here," Vinzant said. Libra and Kandyce gathered on either side. "Looks like the rare books are downstairs."

"All right then," said Libra. "Let's go."

They all jerked their heads at the sound of a creaking door. It was the same one they had used to come in.

"Dammit," whispered Libra. "Guess the goon squad is here."

Vinzant punched his fist into an open palm. "We fightin'?"

Libra felt his heartrate climb at the idea. He'd never at admit to anyone—even himself—that he was afraid of fighting. Despite being good, it was always the last thing he wanted to do. "No. Let's go grab the book and get out quietly."

"You're no fun," he pouted.

They picked up the pace and headed to the nearest door marked with a sign that read *STAIRS*. Once they got down, the smell of old dry books was like a stale perfume, almost like an old construction site. It wasn't as roomy or comfortable as upstairs.

Only a few desks and chairs were present in what served as a waiting room of sorts to the rare books section in the back. Glass walls separated it from where the three of them now stood. They got closer and peered through, ensuring nothing looked out of the ordinary.

"What's the name of this book?" asked Kandyce.

Libra scratched his head. "I don't know, exactly."

"Great. We really don't have time to look through all of these."

The thunderous sound of boots coming down the stairs was a sudden shock that made them all pull out their swords. With their backs against the glass wall, they watched a small entourage of rough-looking people filter into the room. They were fit men and women with either a BAC in their hands or a sword hanging in an over-the-shoulder sheath. One of the women was different. She wore a grey pinstripe suit and had her black dreadlocks pulled into a short ponytail. Her black high heels made a steady knock against each step as she descended.

Vinzant counted, *four...six...eight*! "He needed all of you to find a book?" he exclaimed.

The woman in the suit came down last. She stepped into a small pool of light from a bulb in the ceiling, revealing her brown, almond-shaped face. She said, "We knew there would be a chance we'd run into everyone's favorite hero. And what do you know? The Auctorat plus two!"

"The book is ours," said Libra. "Back down now, and we don't have to fight."

"I'm sorry, that just won't do. I will allow you the same chance."

It looked like he wouldn't be able to avoid fighting after all. "No way."

"Well then," she said, turning to her team. "You know what to do."

Libra looked to his left. "Can you fight, Kandyce?" To which she just huffed out a laugh.

The biggest guy of the group, sword brandished, came after Libra. Libra felt they all came after him. It was as if the accolades of taking down the Auctorat were what they were after more than anything. The woman in the suit stayed back along with another guy who had his BAC drawn as the last line of defense. The other six converged on Libra's team: two for each of them. Libra dodged, blocked sword strikes, and swung back, but he was beginning to feel the pressure. "A little help guys," he cried.

"Kinda dealing with our own stuff, bro," said Vinzant in the middle of a fight all his own.

"Any fire power, Kandyce?"

"My ring's still recharging. It takes a while," she said.

Libra caught his words too late. He had just outed her as an Etherean. After a quick scan of the room to see if anyone heard that little exchange, Libra saw the cold expression of the leader's face change to concern. Anytime ether, or magic, was part of a fight, it became a big threat. She turned to her gunman and pointed at Kandyce, saying, "She's an Etherean." The gunman lowered his sights at Kandyce.

"Kandyce!" Libra warned, "Duck!"

Kandyce saw the man aiming at her and thought fast, grabbing the other man she was fighting off by the shirt and pulling him into the gunman's line of sight. The gun went off in a bang that rang through the room. Its bullet punched a hole in the human shield's back. The force from the shot caused Kandyce's attacker to fall and push her into the glass wall of the rare books section. The glass shattered with the dead man on top of her.

"Kandyce! You okay?" said Libra.

All he got in response were groans, but he could see her moving.

To the other side of Libra, Vinzant parried an attack and countered with a deadly sword strike in his attacker's chest. "One down," he said. He jumped on the wall behind him and lunged at his other attacker with a punch strong enough to knock him out. "That's two, and…" he grabbed his fallen attacker's gun and aimed up to the gunman in the back and shot. "Three! Aren't you glad you have me?" The gunman fell and the woman in the suit jumped aside in a start.

"I'll be even better if you can get one of these two off of me," Libra said. The two he was fighting were a man and a woman. The man was short, but quick. And the woman was tall with a muscular frame. What was surprising was that she hadn't even drawn a weapon. She just used her fists. All she had were long metallic wrist guards as defense. The man would strike with his sword, Libra would block, and the woman would throw a punch. He'd been dodging all of the attacks until now. The short man had broken through Libra's guard and knocked him back a bit. Libra turned to his side and caught his balance, but upon recovering, he felt the woman's fist land hard on his side right below his rib cage. His sword fell to the ground and he let out a scream. He crossed his hands at his face to weakly block the impending next punch. The blow knocked him on the floor. He saved his face, but everything else hurt like a bitch.

Vinzant stepped in and started to fight the man. They were both quick and neither could land a solid hit on the other. Libra looked to his other side and saw another woman jump in after Kandyce, who by then, had pushed the corpse off of herself. He lay still for a moment, trying to catch his breath, but his attacker grabbed him off the ground and said, "Get up!"

Libra regained enough strength to dodge her flurry of attacks and even land few of his own. They had little effect. Her abs were almost as hard as a wall. He eyed his sword on the ground. He'd have to cut her down, if he wanted to survive. "Kandyce, we could use you now."

"On it," she said.

Libra felt relieved at the sight of a red hue coming from her direction. She'd finally recharged her crystal ring, but it was strange. The whole room was bathing in a red light. That couldn't have been just that small ring. Libra snuck a peek behind him and saw one of the books on the shelves was glowing as well, like an ember. Turning back, he noticed the woman in the suit start to move. That must be the book they were all looking for. "Kandyce, the book!"

Kandyce dodged her attacker's strike and cut her down quick. The group's leader was fast approaching. Libra smirked, knowing she was too petite to stand against Kandyce.

Kandyce said, "Where do you think you're going?"

The woman waved a hand to the side and caused a strong gust of wind to knock Kandyce out of her way. "To get what I came for."

Libra's heart sank. She was an air Etherean.

The woman went to the shelf and grabbed the book, but she began screaming. She doubled over and held her burned hand.

Vinzant finally ended his fight and landed a strike on the short man who had gotten distracted by his leader's screams. The shrill sound caused Libra's attacker to pause, giving him a chance to grab his sword. Vinzant came up behind the strong woman and pointed his sword at her neck. Libra did the same at her front. She raised her arms in surrender.

Out the corner of his eye, Libra could see Kandyce wasn't deterred after being knocked away. She got up and used the power of her ring to instantly burst a flame into her hand. She was ready for a fight with magic.

The woman in the suit yelled, "Okay, everybody stop! Stop!" She looked at Kandyce. "It's yours."

The strong woman protested, "But what about Talon?"

"I'll deal with him. I can't take the book. We're done here." She got up and looked at the Auctorat. "Don't think this is over."

She and her last remaining teammate swiftly left up the stairs. Libra was relieved the fight was over. He looked at his new teammates and felt a sense of pride over their success. Maybe there was something to this team thing.

"Who's the sidekick now?" joked Vinzant.

They all gathered themselves and headed through the broken glass wall to the glowing book. Libra looked at Kandyce and said, "It seemed like it reacted to your ether. Think you can pick it up?"

"I can try." She stored her flame back into her ring and reached out. After a couple of cautious taps, she lowered fingers on the top and pulled the book out. No problem. "So, this is what they were after? Why is it protected by fire magic?"

"Guess we'll have to read what's inside," Libra replied. "Kandyce. You think you'd be interested in joining us? We're all after the same guy. We could help each other."

"You kidding? Of course. I'll take all the help I can get to bring that bastard down."

"Good. Let's get out of here and see what's in this book."

CHAPTER EIGHT

I t took a while to work his way in, but Micks was finally hired as one of the servants at the mayor's estate. For the time being, his name was Jefferey. His short, curly black beard, rectangular-rimmed glasses, and blonde dyed hair were a part of his disguise. Mayor Wilhelm was hosting Talon for the night, for a tasty dinner and chat just between the two of them. Micks knew this would be the perfect time to strike with no distractions this time. No Auctorat. Just a quick kill and escape. The money was so close now.

He waited now in front of the Estate for Talon's arrival. He could make out the gate opening in the distance. The twilight had obscured his vision some, but an ornate wheeler came slowly rolling down the drive and around the large fountain in the middle of the cul-de-sac. When it stopped, Micks approached and opened the back-passenger side door. "Good evening, sir," he said as his target stepped out. He closed the door behind him and climbed the few stone steps to the front door to allow Talon entry.

"Where's Wilhelm?" Talon asked, removing his coat.

Micks grabbed the coat and found it hard not to look at Talon's metallic arm. "He should be on his way any minute. May I grab that?" Micks motioned to the glove on Talon's metallic arm.

"No."

"Apologies. May I grab anything for you? A drink?"

"Yes. A drink would be nice. One for the mayor as well, I suppose. The chef knows what we want."

"Right away." After hanging the coat, he led Talon to the dining room and pulled out his chair.

"Please wait here. Mayor Wilhelm will be right down."

Micks made his way straight to the kitchen. He was glad to get away from that man. There was a foreboding presence about him that set him on edge. He felt it the first time when he'd missed his chance at killing him. His instinct told him that he would never be able to take him on in a head-to-head fight. He began to think maybe it was better that he failed the first time. This time would be much quieter.

The clanging of pots grew louder, and the aroma of seasoned chicken and roasted vegetables grew stronger as he got to the kitchen. Beyond the door, the head chef and his sous chef were hard at work preparing the night's meal. While the sous chef was busy on meat and vegetables, the head chef was perfecting a sauce—stirring, tasting, and adding more seasoning. Micks hated to break his concentration, but he leaned on the metal counter between them and spoke up over the loud sizzling of the stove. "Jack! Talon's here. He said you know what drink he likes?"

Jack turned and frowned, furrowing his bushy eyebrows. Micks couldn't get over his tall, athletic stature, his bald head, or the tattoos on his arms under rolled-up sleeves. Micks had a job to do, but boy, Jack made it hard.

"How the fuck should I know?" asked Jack. "I don't do drinks. He's always got me redirecting you guys to the damn bartender," he said. He shared a laugh with his sous chef who was always witness to this. "Go ask her. She knows."

Even his bad language was a turn-on. Micks sighed, sorry for what he was about to do to Jack, his creation, and perhaps his reputation. But, he remembered a deal he'd made with himself long ago to keep his heart out of it and complete his mission. "Got it. Thanks." He headed out the side door to the bartender who immediately poured the drink. It was a hard, brown liquor with an aroma that reached far beyond the glass. Micks returned to see Jack with a look of satisfaction on his face for the perfect sauce. He slowed his step and waited for a chance to make his move.

"You ready to plate?" Jack asked his sous chef. His assistant nodded, and Jack looked behind him for plates, but saw that none of them were there. "Shit. Where are the clean plates? Who was on cleaning duty today?"

Micks spoke up, "I was. Is something wrong?"

"You didn't clean."

"I could have sworn I left some clean dishes for tonight's service. Mayor Wilhelm must have had a bite earlier." He sat the drink down on a nearby counter and came into the cooking area. "There should be some in the cabinet further down, let me—"

"No, it's all right. I'll get them."

Jack turned away, leaving Micks at the stove. With his eye on Jack and his back to the sous chef, he added his own ingredient to the sauce. It was a white, powdery substance he'd stored in a twisted piece of paper earlier in the day. He was glad he had the forethought to leave clean plates a good distance away. This bought him the time he needed. He took a

64

plastic tasting spoon nearby made a quick stir. As Jack returned, he made sure all he saw was the spoon coming down from his lips, pretending to taste.

"The sauce is delicious," said Micks.

Jack just grunted and plated the food, but Micks could tell he appreciated the compliment. Micks grabbed a serving tray for the two plates and drinks. After everything was placed, he hoisted up the circular platform and made his way down the hall and into the dining room. He let out a long sigh of relief before entering. Now, all he had to do was serve and wait.

He sat the food and drinks on table and idled a moment in the corner of the room. Mayor Wilhelm had joined Talon and they were already deep into their conversation.

"So, have you thought any more about what we last talked about?" asked Talon. He grabbed his drink and leaned back in his chair.

"I have and my opinion hasn't much swayed," said Wilhelm. He grabbed his fork and knife and started cutting away at the chicken, drizzled in a *special* sauce.

Micks tilted his head up in anticipation for a bite that would seal the deal. Mayor Wilhelm did not disappoint. He chewed and swallowed the first piece of chicken and went for more. Micks did his best to contain a smile from forming on his lips. He looked at Talon, hoping he would do the same, but he had only touched his drink so far.

"So, you're really going to repeal the tax. Ridiculous," said Talon.

"Well, you didn't let me finish," said Wilhelm, mid-chew. He glanced at Talon's plate. "You gonna eat? Chef Jack is the best."

Talon rested his glass on the table and sat up, ready to eat. He grabbed his utensils and began slowly cutting into meat, all the while keeping his eyes on Wilhelm. "So? Finish."

"Well, I've been doing some research, and I don't think you'll like what I found." He glanced over his shoulder at Micks. "Could you excuse us for a moment, please?"

Micks nodded and left the room but waited just around the corner.

***

Wilhelm leaned in over his food and kept his voice low. "I know your game, Talon."

Talon stopped himself from taking his first bite of dinner and lowered his fork. "What game?"

"This tax. The new university. It's all a ruse, isn't it? Just admit it."

Talon's tone grew hard. "Admit what?"

"That this is all to help your business. To put money in your pockets."

"That's preposterous. My only business is your business. I'm an advisor. Aren't we friends?"

"Are we? How can we be when you've been manipulating me this whole time? Your name is Talbot Stern. You became the black sheep of your noble family after losing your position with the Queen. You own a minor stake in your brother's company, Clearstone, and this tax hurts your competitors and drives consumers straight to your stores just over the city border into Lotus Valley." He covered his mouth and coughed.

Talon sat back. His could feel his temperature rise along with the beating of his heart. He almost couldn't believe it. This boy had really found out. "Where did you get this information?"

"You seem to forget. I'm the mayor. I'm the one with the real power here."

Talon's eyes glazed over at the mention of real power. If he could choke the man right now, he would.

Mayor Wilhelm continued, "It's all good, though, my man." He coughed again, his voice getting strained. "Because you're gonna cut me in." Another cough.

"Cut you in? What about your noble aspirations for the city?"

"The city can wait. They've been suffering this long, what's another…" the coughing came again, but this time it wouldn't stop. Wilhelm's face colored red and the coughing became violent. He fell out of his seat in a thud.

Here's a surprise, Talon thought. His mind raced trying to figure out his next best move. If Wilhelm died, he wouldn't have to live with the threat of being exposed. The only problem was, his proximity to power would die along with him. He'd already had to start over after being fired from Queen Aeothesca's entourage. He didn't want to do that again. Still, the look of horror in Wilhelm's eyes was so amusing that he soaked it in a bit longer before calling for help. He got up from his seat and kneeled on the floor to get into Wilhelm's red, tear-streaked face. "If you make it through this… it's a deal."

***

Micks couldn't make out much of what the men were saying but pretended not to hear a thud. Had it been Talon or the mayor that had fallen? Then, he heard a voice yelling, "Help! Help!" It was Talon's voice. Micks went back into character and sprang into action. He turned the corner into the dining room with a concerned look on his face. It had almost turned into a frown as he saw that Talon had eaten nothing. So much for the bonus. "Oh my God!" he said. Now it was time to make as much commotion as possible and make his escape. He ran through the house yelling, "Someone call an ambulance! It's the mayor! He ate something bad! This is an emergency!" Surely enough, a rush of servers, workers, and some security personnel came toward the dining room. Micks pushed his way through the crowd and brushed against Jack on the way out. He made sure to implant Jack's pocket with his own twisted piece of paper with poison, before leaving.

CHAPTER NINE

"What is this place?" Vinzant asked.

Libra pulled down the aluminum sliding door of the dark warehouse. "It was my father's place when he was alive. Now, it's the Auctorat's hideout."

He caught Kandyce looking around, seeing nothing but a wooden folding table and a few chairs.

"It's so...bare," she remarked.

"Too busy fighting crime to decorate. You're welcome to pitch in though," Libra said with a smile.

"I'll pass. So, this book," said Kandyce, holding it in her hands, "...aside from being protected by magic, what else is special about it? What does it do?"

"It's supposed to be a guide to the location of the Dragon's Bit."

"Dragon's what?"

Libra thought back to his conversation with Micks that day he fought Talon. "You know, like a bit for a horse just…bigger."

Kandyce squinted her eyes at Libra. "Uh-huh…"

Libra raised his hands. "That's just what I was told. Let's take a look."

They all took a seat around the wood table. It had a checkerboard pattern on top, but no game pieces anywhere. Kandyce placed the book in the middle. Its spine showed two lines in gold that met at a point, like triangle cut in half. The book was hard with a worn brown cover and depicted a dragon's head in gold.

Vinzant asked, "I caught you looking at it on the way over. What was it about?"

Kandyce shrugged. "Not much. Something about a fight between two of the elemental spirits. Go ahead, Libra. Open it and look for yourself. It's not going to burn you. It only heats up when my ether is activated."

Libra frowned at the book and reached out to touch it with his fingertips. His instincts made him pull back, but when he felt no heat, he grabbed and opened the small book. It was only a few pages. It told of a fight in old times thousands of years ago during what people now called the Expansion. After a few minutes of reading, Libra said, "It's a historical record. One that was never included in the Sacred Texts, apparently. And since it involves the Spirits of Ether, it should have been."

"What's it about?" asked Vinzant.

"It says back when we were fighting off the Lusae for more land, the fire spirit inhabited a human. Since he had so much power, he forged some sort of artifact that allowed him to call and ride a dragon as his own personal pet. Humans were getting too close to taking over, and the fire spirit used the dragon at a desert settlement—"

"The Middle Desert?"

"I don't know. Maybe. I guess. It says it used the dragon to kill most of the people there but was fought off by another human with control of the earth spirit. Both were badly injured. The human who served as the vessel for the earth spirit died in the desert, but the fire spirit's vessel was taken south by its dragon to die. That's about it."

"Hmm," said Kandyce. "Think maybe the fire spirit's final resting place could be the Incaen Forest?"

"The place that's on fire but never burns out?" Vinzant chimed in. "Sounds like fire spirit type of stuff to me."

"So, this artifact, the Dragon's Bit…why does Talon want it?" asked Kandyce.

"A pet? A takeover? Who knows? In any case, we won't truly know until we get all the pieces together. All we need is something to hold over Talon's head. Something good enough to make him resign. I think we're just about there…unless…our position could be stronger if we had the second book."

Kandyce shook her head. "Wait, a second book? There's another one?"

"It's what the other guy found last time we met. It might be more concrete about the location of the Dragon's Bit."

"Wait a minute, Libra," Vinzant chimed. "You've got one book. If it's that important to Talon, why can't we force him out now?"

"He's got a point," said Kandyce. "It's not like we need the Dragon's Bit."

"I need to be sure this'll work," Libra responded. "I'm not doing anything half-assed. If we leave an opening for Talon to screw us, he will. We need all the leverage. Period."

Libra pretended not to see the disapproving glance shared between his new partners.

"All right," said Kandyce. "But, are we really to believe all this? A dragon and a fire spirit?"

"Doesn't matter. If Talon believes it, then this is our only chance. Plus, we've got a burning book. Something's up, that's for sure."

"Then, we just have to find the other one, right?" said Vinzant.

"Right. We gotta find the double agent. Micks."

CHAPTER TEN

The sunlight showed in a red hue behind Micks' closed eyelids. He turned in his bed to get away from it for a few more minutes of sleep. The night before had been successful, but taxing. His constant repositioning during the night had snapped the edges of his sheets from their snug position under the mattress. He now swam among layers of soft linen and found another position more comfortable. His comfort was shattered when his comm. began to ring. Micks didn't mind. In fact, that was the only thing he welcomed to interrupt his sleep. He knew Mr. Draw would be calling and awaited the news of his payment—enough for a way out of Probuston.

He lifted himself from rest and answered, "Hello, Mr. Draw."

"Is this some kind of joke?"

Micks' heart sank, and his anticipation died at his employer's tone. "What do you mean? What happened?"

"'Mayor Wilhelm is alive and well after an attack by his own chef who is now in the custody of the Enforcers'. It says so right here in today's news."

Micks almost dropped his comm. He gripped it harder in disbelief and felt himself start to tremble. He couldn't tell whether to feel fear or rage. Mr. Draw must have been trying to get out of payment. It just couldn't be true. "Mr. Draw, that can't be possible."

"Turn on your monitor, son."

"Just a minute." He left his comm. on the bed. The sunlight and warm air through the window at his bedside felt like nothing to him now. He didn't even feel his bare feet hit the splintery wooden floor on his way to the table. Leaning against the back of a wooden chair, he grabbed a remote control, pressed *on*, and watched as the sounds and words of the day's new confirmed what Mr. Draw had said. He went back to his comm. and said, "Mr. Draw…I—"

"We're done."

"If you just give me another chance, I know I can—"

"We're done!"

The line went dead. Micks' frustration turned to raw anger which began to bubble over. He threw his comm. to the ground so hard, it cracked into pieces. "Shit!" He gritted his teeth and found the ability to breathe a moment later. "Shit." With both hands, he grabbed the back of the chair that sat by the table. All of his weight was pressed against it as he bowed his head. *Why?* he wondered. *Why couldn't I make it happen? All of that time wasted. All of that energy. For what?*

And then he thought about Jack. He had framed him for the mayor's murder which was now what the news called an 'attempted assassination'. His anger morphed into guilt. Maybe if he'd been successful and gotten the money, he would have felt better. But, the more he thought about it, he knew that wasn't true. Framing Jack for killing the mayor would have left a mark on his soul that would never go away. In a way, he felt relieved. Maybe this was a chance to set things right. He lifted his head and looked to the shelf just over the monitor. The book he'd grabbed after his first run-in with the Auctorat was sitting there with its spine facing out. An idea began to form. Jack had to be set free; there was no doubt about that. But, as far as getting enough money to start a new life, perhaps there was another person who'd be willing to pay a pretty penny for what he had.

CHAPTER ELEVEN

I

Libra waited in the alley at night as his informant grabbed the data he needed on Micks. He had his usual bandana tied around his face and presented himself as the Auctorat for this meeting. He leaned on the brick wall of the opposite building in the shadow of the street lamp above. The side door to the Enforcers' HQ creaked open and his informant stepped out. "Did you get anything?" Libra asked.

"A little. Not much. His full name is Micayah Wreed. Here's his address." She handed over the thin folder bent inside out. Only two sheets of paper were in the file. One for his name and address, and the other for his service record. She continued, "Apparently, he was a warrior for the Southern Third for some time. Although, that was years ago. There's no record of employment after, no family... It's strange. This would fool anyone at first glance to think he was just a law-abiding citizen. We have record of everyone in the city, and those who don't cause problems have files just as scant as these. But, to not have any record of family or place of birth...it had to have been altered."

"But only an Enforcer has access to that system..."

She raised an eyebrow. "Spoken as though you have some experience."

Libra caught her inquisitive gaze but said nothing. He could tell she was fishing for information on his identity. She wouldn't get any.

"In any case, there's no way he had access to our system," she continued.

"You'd be surprised."

"Oh, really?"

"Yeah. This guy infiltrated Talon's gang."

"The XN?"

"Yeah. And tried to kill Talon. Any Enforcers here gone missing?"

She scrunched her nose and placed her hand under her chin. "There was some story about an Enforcer who went crazy and deserted us to go live with the lusae. It's supposed to have happened years ago. Before I started here. I always thought it was something meant to scare the new recruits. You don't think…"

Libra shrugged, "Could be. He seems to have a way of getting into places that should be closed off."

"You should talk."

"What do you mean?"

"The Grand Library. Six members of the XN were found dead inside. No trace of their killers."

Libra swallowed. "Probably one of their own."

She squinted. "Uh-huh."

He could feel her suspicion of him. They were on good terms, but she was still an Enforcer. He had to be careful. "Thanks for the info, Geneva." He closed the folder and handed it back to her.

"Yeah. And Auctorat…"

"Yeah?"

"No killing. Don't turn into one of those thugs. You find trouble, do what you have to, but no more blood on the streets."

"…sure," he said. He couldn't make any promises, but he had to say something.

II

Late after midnight, Libra showed up at the address marked in Micks' file. The neighborhood wasn't the best, but the same could be said for the whole city, just about.

It was an apartment building and apparently Micks lived on the third floor. The only problem was getting in. The front door was protected by a passcode. He could wait for a tenant to come by and open it, but he doubted anyone would let in a man in a bandana. There had to be another way. He went around the side of the building where he found the fire escape. The only problem was that it was blocked by a tall gate, chained in the middle, and secured by a padlock. Good thing he had his sword. As he took a hard swing and destroyed the chain, he hoped the sound wasn't loud enough to wake anybody up. He waited a moment. After hearing no commotion nor seeing any lights turn on, he proceeded up with a daring step on the wall, a twist, and then he clung to the dangling ladder at the bottom. The ladder slid to the ground from his weight, and Libra hoisted himself up and proceeded up to the third floor.

The window had been left open, and as Libra stepped in, it seemed as though no one was home. He looked down in response to the sound of shattered pieces of plastic he kicked while walking around. A broken comm. laid there. Somebody must have been upset. And it sucked because now, if he learned Micks' number, he had no way of getting in touch with him.

Libra came with the intention of asking Micks for his help, but maybe things had turned out for the better. He was in his apartment, so maybe Micks had left the other book that would solve the mystery of the Dragon's Bit.

He could hear the faint sound of sirens in the distance, but aside from that, all was quiet. After checking the shelves and looking under the bed, Libra realized he had no luck. That's when his comm. rang.

He took it out of his pocket and lifted it to his ear, saying, "I thought I told you not to call me unless it was important."

"Chill out, man. It is important," said Vinzant. "There's been a prison break. Check the news."

Libra looked on the table and found the remote control. After turning on the monitor, he saw an aerial view of the prison. The camera was following two dark figures. When they stepped into the light, Libra was surprised to recognize someone. "That's him!"

"Who?"

"Micks! That's him and some prisoner he's breaking out. Wait. Isn't that the guy who tried to kill the mayor?"

"What! That's the guy you're after and he's breaking out an assassin? This is too much."

"Vinzant, I need your help. And Kandyce."

"What? Why? What are you planning?"

"We're going to stop them and get that second book."

III

Micks grabbed ahold of Jack's hand and pulled him around the corner and away from the light of the drone. Because it was shaped like the smallest version of a supertrop, some called it a microtrop. No windows and no passengers, just a large light and a camera.

"Dammit," said Micks.

"They saw my face. They're really gonna come after us now."

"Don't worry, Jack, I'm gonna get you out of this."

"Why? Why are you doing this? What's in this for you?"

Micks stopped scanning his surroundings for a moment and turned to look Jack in the eye. *He really doesn't recognize me,* he thought in a mix of relief and melancholy. He had shaved off the beard, buzz cut his blonde hair back down to black, and wasn't using glasses. He was no longer the waiter at the mayor's estate that Jack knew. It was better that way. Jack would hate him if he knew what he did, but he couldn't help but wish there was a way he could come clean. This was the next best thing. "I know you didn't try to assassinate the mayor."

"How do you know that?"

"I just do." Micks went back to surveying the landscape. Their backs were against a stone wall. The front gate was a no-go. Their only choice was to climb up over the side, but it was a long way down. He spied a guard tower in the distance. That's how he got in. If he could just get back to the tower without getting caught by the drone, they could climb back down safely.

"You know I'm going to need a little bit more than that, right?"

"Well for starters, I'm Micks. But, let's just get out of here first."

Three guards in black body armor rounded the corner and flanked them: two on one side and one on the other.

"Can you fight?" asked Jack.

"I'm the one with the sword. I should be asking you."

"I'm damn good, hand to hand. Your gun would help now, though."

Micks tossed his BAC and they stood back-to-back facing their enemies. Everyone was still in the darkness until the drone came around the corner and shined a light on their position. Jack shot, just missing the guard, but giving him enough time to charge and utilize his strength to pummel him. Micks charged the other two, but the force from a bullet in his chest knocked him back.

"Hey! Micks!" yelled Jack. "Shit."

Hearing Jack call his name like that almost brought a smile to his face, but he played dead a little longer until the guards got closer. He was always prepared with his own armor when on a mission. The bruise would be big, but he had no time to think about the pain. When he saw the guards get closer, Micks sprung back to life. He knocked out one guard with a kick to his chin and parried the swing of the other's sword, giving him enough time to wrap his arm around his neck. The guard eventually stopped struggling and lay unconscious at Micks' feet.

90

"I thought you were a goner," said Jack. "That was nice!"

Micks smiled. Compliments were rare in his line of work but hearing it from Jack made it even more special. "Thanks. Let's get out of here."

They just started to move, but a voice stopped them in their tracks. "I hate to say this, but you're not going anywhere."

"Great," said Jack. "Who the fuck is this?"

"The Auctorat…and friends," Micks responded. "Hey, Auctorat. Long time, no see. I take it you're not here to help us?"

"What are you doing, Micks?"

Micks pointed at Jack over his shoulder. "He's innocent. What are you doing here?"

"I stop crime. And that's what this is. Plus, you have something I need."

"And what is that?"

"Remember that book you picked up last time? We need it."

"Let us go and you can have it," he bluffed. As the words passed his lips, Micks started strategizing about how to renege on that deal.

"Or, I could just pick it up from the Enforcers after they put you back behind these walls."

"You really think the police are going give that to you? Talon's police?"

"Maybe we could just take it from you now." The Auctorat glanced at the woman next to him whose ring glowed a bright red. Micks was shocked to see her hand burst into a controlled flame. He looked at Jack to see the same expression on his face.

"Might want to hand it over now," she said, "...unless you like to feel the burn."

A large flame shot up behind the Auctorat and his entourage just beyond the tower. It looked as though a tree caught fire. The book!

A moment passed in silence while Micks laughed. "Good thing it's not on me."

Micks had been waiting for the perfect moment to attack. The place where he'd stashed the book was blown, but the sudden spike in fire gave Micks and Jack the distraction they needed for a preemptive strike.

Micks swung like crazy to knock the Auctorat off balance, but the element of surprise barely worked as the Auctorat blocked all of his attacks. Jack fended off the other two. His size alone made him a harder fight, but he was surprisingly quick and agile. After knocking the woman back, he swung around and wrapped his muscled arm around the long-haired guy's neck. "Stop or he's dead!"

Micks pointed his blade at the Auctorat who just raised his arms in response. "I'm telling the truth. He's innocent. Don't we have the same enemy? Why are we fighting?"

"You can't break out a prisoner. There's laws and a process—"

"Wake up, Auctorat! We're living in a corrupt system. You know this. You better learn who your enemies are and stop wasting time." Micks kept his blade up as he walked around behind Jack and backpedaled toward the tower. The Auctorat's eyes betrayed his posture. Micks could tell he'd gotten through. "Come on, Jack."

Jack dropped the long-haired man and followed Micks to the tower.

"Wait!"

Micks turned to see the Auctorat jogging after him. "What?"

"Your apartment is being spied on by now. You could use a place to hide. And we really need that book."

Micks frowned. First, he wondered how he knew about his apartment. The more pressing issue, however, was his need for the book. If Talon and the Auctorat were both after it, it had to be even more valuable than he'd expected. He had to learn more. "Okay. We go with you."

"Good." He turned and called the woman's name while pointing at the drone. She burned it in a tiny explosion and caught up along with the man. "Follow me."

***

Libra led the five of them down the stairs of the tower but stopped when he saw a familiar face standing by the door. "Geneva," he said. He felt ashamed. He had been caught by his only friend in the Enforcers.

"Is this what the Auctorat does?" she asked.

"No, Geneva. This is different—"

"You're not who I thought you were." Her eyes were wide, and Libra sensed her fear. He hated it. What he hated even more was that he had been the one to cause it.

"You have to trust me—"

"Just go! You're lucky I came over here on a hunch. I'm calling for backup though. They'll be here soon. I may not see your face, but I'll remember everyone else's."

The air went out of the room with that truth. Suddenly, Libra felt much more responsible for Kandyce and Vinzant. He moved past Geneva to the door outside and whispered, "Sorry."

CHAPTER TWELVE

I

About ten minutes after returning to the warehouse, Libra decided to kill the uneasiness between all of them. Vinzant and Kandyce were seated around the small wood table, and Jack and Micks were sitting on the ground by the wall next to the front door. They were silent, but when Libra approached, Micks got up and met him midway.

"You guys okay?" asked Libra.

"Yeah." Micks looked back at Jack who was deep in his own thoughts. "I think so."

"Where's the book?"

Micks reached in his bag and took it out. Libra reached to take it, but Micks pulled it back. "You still keeping your identity a secret? I think we're all on the same side, now."

Libra pulled at his bandana and hesitated. Not too long ago nobody knew who he was. Nowadays, it seemed like the worst kept secret. He wanted to keep his disguise on, but knew he had to build trust with Micks and Jack. Libra exhaled and removed his bandana. "I'm Libra. That's Kandyce and Vinzant," he said, pointing over at the table.

"Thanks. I'm sure you all already know about us."

Libra received the book from Micks and nodded. "Yeah."

Libra inspected the book and saw that it was almost identical as the one picked up at the Grand Library. It was small with a brown hardcover and a golden illustration of a dragon's head. The binding showed the first half of a triangle at its center. This was definitely the companion to the other book. They had everything they needed to force Talon, and maybe even the mayor, to resign. *However*, Libra pondered. He began to think of how to make his plan even better. *Should we get the Dragon's Bit for ourselves?*

"There's nothing much in there," said Micks. "Just a map and something about a test."

"A test?" Libra thumbed through the book and saw that he was right. A lot of blank pages were on either side of the map drawn in the middle with words at the bottom. Libra read them aloud: "'To control a dragon requires the power of fire. Furthermore, one must take the test. Failure is the end. Power is the beginning.' So that's it. Talon wants control of a dragon, no doubt."

Vinzant shrugged. "I don't know what that is, but it sounds like you need a fire Etherean to even go for it."

"Well, we have one."

"But it says, 'Failure is the end,'" said Kandyce. "I don't know if I like the sound of that."

"But if the 'answers of old' refers to the story in the second book, we have all the answers."

Jack spoke up from the far wall. "Sorry to interrupt, but what do you need a dragon for?"

Libra calmed himself. The discovery had been exciting, but with both books the Dragon's Bit would practically be Talon's. That should be enough. "You're right. We have all the leverage we need. With this, we can force Talon's resignation…maybe get him to convince the mayor to step down, too."

"So, that's what you guys are doing?" said Jack. "Trying to topple the government?"

"Not topple it. Just get rid of some bad eggs who are bringing the city down. Why do you ask? I didn't think you'd be with them, trying to kill the mayor and all—"

"I didn't! I'm innocent."

"That's what they all say."

Jack stood up quick. "Look! I'm a chef, not a fuckin' politician. I know what's going on out here. I want them gone just as much as you do, but I wouldn't kill anyone."

Micks stepped in between them to cut the tension. He reached up to Jack's shoulder and held on. "All right, guys. Maybe we should sleep on it."

Libra took a deep breath. He didn't like having criminals around him. Something in his gut told him not to trust Micks either, but what choice did he have now? He knew he would have to make some hard decisions when he had decided to leave the Enforcers and do his own thing. "Yeah, you're probably right. I guess everybody's sleeping here tonight." He noticed Micks' flirtatious posture as he leaned into Jack with a firm grip on his shoulder. "Are you two…?"

"Oh no," said Micks. "Hardly know the guy."

"Oh. I was going to say you two could sleep together over there, but…"

"I'm fine here," said Jack. He went back to sit in his corner. "He can take the mattress."

Libra noticed a change in Micks' expression. Almost like hurt or disappointment at a lost opportunity. Micks quickly shook it off and said, "Yeah. That works."

II

Micks woke up early the next morning. He thought he had been the first to rise, but saw Libra sitting by the table in deep thought. "Good morning, Libra," he said, joining him at the opposite side.

Libra shook from his stillness. "Oh, hey. Mornin'."

The two sat in silence for a moment. Micks entered a stillness of his own. He thought of his next move. Despite failing his last mission, he was still determined to get out of Probuston with a hefty sum in his pockets. He was also glad he had freed Jack, but hated that he'd made a mess of his life. A plan had already formulated in his mind about how to fix everything last night. The only thing was, he didn't know if he was prepared to execute it. Especially if it meant betraying the man who had saved him and Jack last night.

"Thanks for the book," said Libra.

Micks shrugged. "It was an even exchange. Thanks for helping us."

"So, what are you guys gonna do now? You're wanted men."

"I don't suppose you have room for two more on your team? The other two are on the list as well. We could stick together. Help each other out."

Libra opened his lips but hesitated to produce any words.

"I know, you don't want any criminals on your team," Micks continued, rolling his eyes. "You know, I was the one who told you all about Talon's plan in the first place. You saw what I can do. You could use me. And Jack's a good guy…and a great fighter, as you saw."

Still no answer. Micks huffed and shook his head. Who knew the Auctorat was such a hard head? Just as he got up to leave, Libra stopped him with a question: "How do you know Jack didn't try to kill the mayor?"

"What?"

"You keep saying he's innocent. How do you know?"

Micks sighed. He thought of all the ways to color the truth, but knew he'd lose his chance at safety if he didn't come clean. "Because it was me. I was hired to kill him and Talon."

Libra smiled wryly. "So, you framed Jack for the fall?"

"It was the only way to make a clean escape. If authorities found their murderer, they wouldn't need to search for the waiter who disappeared." He endured Libra's silent judgment before saying, "Look, I feel awful about the whole thing. And I'm done with that life. That's why I broke Jack out. I want to make things right."

Libra took it all in with a deep breath. "Is that everything?"

"That's everything. And like I said, we're here now. Might as well use us."

Libra looked away and gave his words some thought. "You're right," he said. "I have to admit, you've been more than helpful. If anything goes wrong with negotiations, I could use all the help I can get." He stuck out his hand to seal it with a shake.

Micks was surprised at his sudden change of heart and shook on the offer. "Oh, and just…please don't tell Jack. Let me handle that myself."

Libra nodded. "All right."

He was grateful to Libra but knew he would never fully gain his trust. And because of that, he steeled his resolve to put his plan into action. Being a part of the group was temporary. Living like a king in the Middle Third was what he kept his eye on. He had the location of the books and the Auctorat's true identity. He was going to offer Talon some information he was sure he'd pay for.

CHAPTER THIRTEEN

icks found that getting inside Talon's place wasn't very hard. He'd successfully dodged the eyes of the Enforcers on the street and flew under the radar amongst the hustle and bustle of the city. A short cab ride later, he was in the suburb of Lotus Valley where Talon called home.

He knew the drill. Find some unsuspecting worker, knock them out, and trade places. It was a classic move, but only for temporary situations. Infiltrating the mayor's estate and the XN gang required some extra preparation. He only needed a word with the man at the top.

He grabbed the tray of tea the butler left behind off the counter and saw the glass balcony door was open. Talon was sitting at the table and reading. Micks drew in a deep breath and stepped outside.

"Your tea, sir," he said, laying down the tray.

Talon made a quick swing of his metal arm and caught Micks by the neck. "Who are you?"

Micks was stunned. The pressure of Talon's grip against his esophagus allowed him little ability to breathe. The sharp fingertips threatened to break the skin.

Talon stood while pulling Micks to his knees. Slowly, he said again, "Who are you?"

Through gasps of breath Micks managed to say, "I know...about the Dragon's Bit." Talon let him go and he gave a few hard coughs, welcoming the relief of air entering his lungs.

"What do you know about the Dragon's Bit?"

"I only know who has the books you were looking for."

Talon smirked. "Please…"

"Two books about a dragon and their bindings reveal a triangle."

"The symbol of fire. So, you have seen them."

"Yes."

"And who has them?"

"The Auctorat."

"The Auctorat? Dammit. That's no good. I need a name."

"I have a name."

"Out with it."

Micks smiled in spite of himself. "Not before you do something for me."

"What do you want?"

"First, I'll need you to get the mayor to drop the charges against his chef, Jack Valor. And get the Enforcers off my back for breaking him out."

Talon gave a skeptical squint of the eyes. "Is that it?"

"And two million credits. Half up front, the rest when I give you your information."

"Ah! I knew there was more."

"What do you say?"

"You're asking for one million now, and another when you come back? That's too much."

Micks was taken aback. "Surely, for you—"

"Not too much for me. Too much for you. One can do plenty with one million, but how do I know you won't cut and run? I can give you a quarter of it now. Another five hundred thousand in exchange for the information, and the rest after I see that your information is good."

Micks threw out his hand. "Sounds like a deal."

Talon ignored the formality and walked past him into the house. "Wait here."

Micks withdrew his attempt at a handshake. He saw Talon was not one to equate himself with anyone he saw lower. Despite the brief disrespect and his near-death by suffocation, Micks felt charged. Five hundred thousand credits! He'd never had that much at one time in his life. And it had been so easy.

Talon's footsteps snapped him back to attention. He was surprised by the thud of a brown leather bag being thrust into his chest. He unzipped the top and felt the edges of his cheeks stretch in an uncontrollable smile. It was full of banknotes. Credits. He had hit pay dirt.

"Five hundred thousand. It's all there," said Talon. He sat back in his chair and went back to reading. "I'll do my part. And, I'll expect you to do yours."

Micks' excitement threatened to erode into paranoia. Talon didn't seem like a person you'd easily get away from, even after completing a job. He hoped he hadn't gotten in over his head. Micks took another look inside of the bag and fought off the nerves. If it ever came down to it, he knew could defend himself. For now, he was going to celebrate. He began to walk away from Talon but was stopped by his voice.

"Oh, and untie the real butler, will you? Tell him I need another pot of tea. This one's gone cold."

CHAPTER FOURTEEN

I

Talon was led into the mayor's study by a new doorman. A fleeting thought about the man who came to see him that morning passed through his head. Something about that experience bothered him as he thought of the new doorman.

"What do you want, Talon?" said Mayor Wilhelm.

Talon watched as he rounded the corner from the dining room in a wheelchair. It beeped and whirred as his fingers pressed the touchpad on the armrest. He was a sickly pale. The only color in him were the yellowish bags under his eyes. The kindness in his voice had never returned since that day.

Not that Talon cared. "I need to speak to you. We have an opportunity."

"We? After the way you spoke to me?" His chair made a smooth turn away from Talon and went down the wide hallway toward the back terrace.

Talon followed with a brisk pace. "You aren't over that yet?"

"You waited for me to die, Talon." Wilhelm moved outside onto the stone terrace with tall lamps on either side that illuminated the area in the night sky. Plenty a party had been hosted here, and even now, Talon tried to lead a dance of sorts with his young charge.

"I'm telling you about an opportunity for the both of us and you want to throw that in my face?"

Wilhelm stopped. For a long moment, he sat in silence.

Talon stood behind him and smiled. Emotional blackmail always worked on Wilhelm.

Wilhelm turned to face Talon. "What is it you came to tell me?"

"We're going to make you Commander of the Southern Third."

"What are you talking about? Do I look like I'm in shape for a Power Battle?"

"Oh, there will be no need for Power Battles anymore."

"I don't like where this is going."

"Hear me out. I've been working on a passion project, if you will. I've been searching for the Dragon's Bit."

"Dragon's Bit?"

"It's an artifact that allows you control of a dragon."

Wilhelm rolled his eyes and stifled a laugh. "Okay, and have you found it?"

"Not quite. You need a pair of books to reveal its location."

"And you've found the books?"

"Yes...kind of. A gentleman came to see me today. He told me he knows of the books' whereabouts."

"So, why don't you go get them?"

"They're in the possession of the Auctorat."

Wilhelm's brows jumped at mention of the city's hero. "I see."

"Right. And nobody knows his identity."

"Except this man who came to see you."

"Correct. He said he's willing to release his identity, but he needs you to do something."

"Me? What?"

"Drop the charges against Jack Valor and the man who broke him out of custody."

Wilhelm touched the pad on his wheelchair and began to move back inside with a roll of his eyes and a huff. "Goodnight, Talon."

"Wait!"

Wilhelm stopped and turned. "You want me to let that murderous chef go free? After what he did? Look at me, Talon! I'm in a fucking chair and you want to go dragon hunting?"

"Everything I said is true! If you would stop trying to make me feel stupid, you would see. This is it! I spent plenty of time in the library at Lorelei Castle. You have no idea what is out there. This man has the books and I am certain, with a dragon, we can make our move."

Wilhelm made a sound somewhere between a laugh and a cough. "So, you want to take over the country with a dragon. What you're saying is treasonous… Even if this thing exists, what if I don't want to be commander?"

Talon laid a hand on Wilhelm's shoulder and leaned in. He knew he was going to get the mayor on his side. "You really don't want to be the leader of the nation?" Wilhelm looked away and Talon stood back up. It was time to give up the information he'd hoarded. "The Queen is an Etherean."

Wilhelm's wandering gaze snapped back to Talon. He could see he was telling the truth.

"I was there during the war. The rumors are true. She cracked open the earth and sunk scores of warriors, including your father and your brother."

"Why have you never told me this?"

"The code I lived by as a noble and an advisor to the Queen is hard to shake. But as loyal as I was to her, I will be to you. I know what this man said is true. These books will lead us to the Dragon's Bit. And once we have it, we can get out of this city, into the capitol, and get back at that woman in the castle. So, a chef tried to kill you. So what? You're alive. What legacy will prosecuting him leave behind? Whatever you need, I will guide you through, and you will be known as the greatest commander who ever lived."

Wilhelm exhaled and bent over in his chair with a pained expression, but Talon could see it was not physical. It was emotional. Wilhelm wanted Jack's head on a stake badly, but by reading his expression, Talon could tell he made the painful decision to stay short-term satisfaction for long-term glory.

Talon found a spot of shadow, just outside of the lamp's light. It was the perfect spot to hide a wide grin.

II

It had been a few days since Micks made the deal with Talon. Already, his nerves were on edge. With the money he'd gotten, he thought he would go celebrate and buy something expensive, but his guilt got in the way. Instead, he had returned to the warehouse, bag of money discreetly hanging from his shoulder. But not before making a stop.

He had decided his first purchase would be a way to thank the Auctorat and his team for providing him and Jack a place to stay. So, he went to the furniture store and ordered a few mattresses and plenty of linens. Upon their delivery, the smiles and gratitude he received had only made him feel worse. *What have I done?* he thought. He tried to kill the regret with the thoughts of what was before him: a simpler, peaceful...*rich* life in a new city. And repeated his mantra to himself, never to let his heart get in the way.

Today, he only found momentary relief from the announcement in the news. He sat at the table alone and watched as Libra trotted in from a short trip to see his mother. He had a strange look on his face and Micks didn't know what to make of it. He soon found out that it had everything to do with the newspaper that was in his hand.

"Jack," he said, "...it seems I was wrong about you."

Everyone had been in different corners of the room, biding their time until they found a way from under the Enforcers' pursuit. When Libra slapped the paper on the table, everyone perked up and crowded around. Micks saw the headline first and saw that for once, his plan had worked. It read, ALL CHARGES DROPPED: JACK VALOR GOES FREE. He shared a knowing glance with Libra, grateful that he still played ignorant. While Libra knew Micks was to blame for Jack's arrest, he didn't know that Micks was to blame for his freedom. Micks kept that bit of information to himself.

Jack was last to the table. He stared at the paper and picked it up in disbelief. After a moment, he broke the silence with a laugh.

"Way to go, big guy," said Vinzant. "What do you think happened?"

Jack was still in a state of shock. "I don't know... It'll be hell trying to restore my reputation, but I'll take it."

Libra said, "It says that the Enforcers found evidence that ruled out Jack's involvement. What exactly that is, it doesn't say, but who cares? You're free."

Seeing the smile on Jack's face let Micks know that he had done something right. It felt good and he hoped he could take that feeling with him into the next phase of the deal. He didn't like Talon. And maybe Talon didn't really need the Auctorat's name like he said. *What if I only give him the information in the books*, Micks wondered. That way, Talon could get the Dragon's Bit for himself. He had to try.

III

Once the excitement of Jack's freedom died down, Libra addressed the group: "So, how do we feel about the plan to negotiate Talon's resignation with these books?"

"The same as before," said Vinzant. "You ready to do it?"

Libra twisted his mouth. "Not really. I just don't know about it." He noticed he was missing someone. "Wait, where's Micks?"

"He said he had something to take care of," said Jack.

"Oh, I guess we'll fill him in later."

Back on topic, Kandyce asked, "So, what's not to know? About the plan? We have all the leverage."

"Do we, though?" said Libra. "The books are not the Dragon's Bit which is what Talon really wants. I just feel we're leaving ourselves vulnerable somehow."

Kandyce raised an eyebrow. "You really think he'd pass on a deal to have concrete info on the Dragon's Bit?"

"No, but he could manipulate everything and turn it against us. Let's say we approach him with this deal. He could say, 'I need to verify that the Dragon's Bit even exists,' or 'I need to make sure it's still there.' This forces us to give him the books first, so he can verify. After that, we have no way of knowing whether he'll hold up his end of the bargain. In all that time spent verifying, he'd have come up with a plan to screw us over and gain even more power."

"Libra's got a point," said Jack. "The only way to get something out of powerful people is to give them something of value. It's how I found my mentor years ago. I offered to work for free and he showed me everything he knew about the culinary world. If you want Talon to step down without a fight, you have to give him exactly what he wants upfront so that there are no other options."

"And then take it away," said Libra.

Jack shrugged. "That's up to you. I just know I've gotta go home. Try to rebuild my life and restore my reputation. I hope I can." He shook hands with everyone as his goodbye.

Libra clapped him on the shoulder. Libra understood his need to go back to his life, but a selfish part of him wanted Jack to stay. "Good luck, man. You've always got a spot here if you need it."

"Thanks," Jack replied. "I appreciate that. Good luck, guys. Be safe."

And with that, Jack left.

"So, are we planning a trip to go get the Dragon's Bit ourselves?" asked Vinzant.

Libra nodded. "Looks like it."

CHAPTER FIFTEEN

I

"You've returned," said Talon without turning from his chair.

Micks approached him at his usual spot on the balcony. This time the tea was hot. "I have, Talon. I have to say, I'm surprised you got it done so quickly. Thank you."

"Who is the Auctorat?"

Micks thought he'd be able to finesse Talon away from the topic, but he got straight to the point. Micks still had to try. "Why don't we start with what's necessary to find the Dragon's Bit? I know what's in the books."

Talon placed his book on the table and turned to face Micks. "What do they say?"

"You have to visit the final resting place of the fire spirit and undergo its test."

"What kind of test?"

"I don't know. I just know it could be life-threatening. The other book tells the story of the ancient vessel, his last human form, and how he got the dragon, as well as his end. I can tell you the story—"

"The Auctorat knows all of this, correct?"

Micks swallowed. "Yeah."

"And his name? That was the deal, uh…" he searched for a name.

"Micks."

"Yes well, out with it."

Micks felt the air escape him. He'd tried to spare the only people who had shown him some kindness in this city. He steeled himself, remembering the money on the line. Five hundred thousand credits just for giving up this information. *Put your heart away,*

Micks, he said to himself. "His name is Libra. Libra Alexander."

Talon smiled. "Very good. The butler has your money. You'll get the rest when I see that this information checks out. Good day." He turned back to his book; done with the conversation.

"Good day, sir."

Micks sustained an evil glare from the butler he'd subdued the other day as he grabbed his money. He didn't open it to check the amount. He just walked out of the house with his head hung low. Micks had a bad feeling about what was to come for Libra.

II

After getting his team into such a mess, Libra felt it necessary to at least stay with them at the warehouse. Jack was a free man and had returned home. Micks was off doing his own thing, but made contact from time to time to check on preparations for the trip. They were okay. But Kandyce and Vinzant were still on the Enforcers' radar. They didn't deserve to be. Libra needed to find a way to make it right.

He had been spending less time at home, but still came in to check on his mother every day. Today was no different. Except it was entirely different. He walked up the three stone steps to his front door and pulled out his key to unlock it. When he raised it to the door, he saw that there was no need; a small breeze had caused it to swing open. He thought it was strange and questioned if he had forgotten to lock it on his way out last night. Then, he felt hopeful that his mother was actually up and about, back to her old self. He moved inside and closed the door behind him. His insides tensed when he saw the living room in shambles. The monitor had been knocked to the floor, as had all of his mother's glass knick-knacks. And his mother wasn't on the couch.

"Mom?" Libra stepped over the shattered remains of tchotchkes and called again, "Mom?"

He told himself to breathe. One of the skills he'd picked up as an Enforcer was to calm himself under pressure. He figured she could just be upstairs, but ignored the nagging paranoia that she'd been attacked.

Upstairs, he went from room to room. "Mom? Mom? Say something!" He could feel his calm beginning to break. "Please…"

Outside, he thought. The door had been open. *She must be outside*. He ran back downstairs, through the living room, and out the front door. "Mom!" he yelled. His boots squished against the dewy grass as he ran to the back of the house. "Mom!" His breathing began to catch up to the pace of his fast heartbeats. She was nowhere to be found.

He ran back into the house and stood in the living room. The idea that she had been attacked

126

finally became real. He squatted and held his face, reddened with fear and dampened with tears. What had happened? How had he not been able to protect what was most precious to him?

He moved his hands from his face to the top of his skull, brushing back strands of hair from his view. His mind raced for any clue, anything he had missed, desperate for some answer as to what was going on. When he noticed a blank envelope on the couch, he lunged at it. He flipped open the back and pulled out the sheet of paper inside. It was a short, handwritten letter. One line, but enough to shake him back to rage:

The Dragon's Bit for the Auctorat's mother.

— Talon

As far as Libra was concerned, Talon was a dead man.

CHAPTER SIXTEEN

I t was just the three of them. Libra, Vinzant, and Kandyce sat around the wooden table in the warehouse. Libra had just dropped the news.

"Your mom, bro?" said Vinzant. "That's messed up."

"Your mother, my girlfriend… Who's next?" asked Kandyce. "Talon is a monster."

Libra sat back in his chair with a frown and crossed his arms over his chest. He agreed with everything they said, but hated the feeling of regret. "We waited too long." He sat up and leaned over the table with his elbows, his clasped hands supporting his forehead. "I waited too long," he corrected. "We had the leverage and let it slip through our fingers. I'm so sorry, guys."

Kandyce scooted her chair over and laid a hand on his shoulder. "You have nothing to be sorry about. We just have to adjust. Any chance at negotiating him and Wilhelm out of power are gone. So, what's next?"

Libra looked up at Kandyce. "I don't think we have a choice."

The entrance to the warehouse opened, and a voice shouted in, "Don't get to the good part without us!"

"Micks?" said Libra, surprised. "What are you doing here?"

"My intuition told me you may need a hand. I brought Jack with me." Jack followed in behind Micks.

"You too, Jack?"

"They took everything," Jack said. His voice was low and morose. "My house was ransacked, money stolen. I doubt I'll ever get a job as a chef in this city again." He shook his head and shoulders as if his mood were an annoying child trying to get his attention. "What's the plan with Talon? You get the artifact yet?"

"That's actually what we were discussing," said Kandyce. "Libra…" she looked at the wounded Auctorat for his approval to tell the story. "Libra's mother was kidnapped by Talon."

Jack's shock was as expected, but Libra was almost brought out of his panic by Micks's reaction. He stepped back, mouth agape, with his hands searching for something to hold his balance. Jack stuck out a hand to keep him up. "Libra…" said Micks. "I'm so sorry. I didn't know—"

"You didn't know what?"

Micks stepped away from Jack and sat in the last remaining seat around the table. "I-I didn't know that Talon was capable of something like this."

"Are you kidding?" Libra sensed that there was something more, something he was missing. "Do you know anything about this, Micks?"

Micks recoiled. "Me? No! It's just… Your mother? I just hate that this has happened to you. Same as everyone else."

Libra took a deep breath. "I'm sorry. It's just that I was so careful about my identity for this reason. And nobody but us knew."

"And you immediately look at me?"

"I don't mean to be suspicious, but I know about you, Micks. And what I do know is that there isn't much to know, thanks to you."

Micks huffed. "You sure you were never followed? That bandana you use isn't much of a disguise. Someone might have recognized you."

Libra nodded at each point. "I'm sorry. Really. I'll need all the help I can get now."

Micks took a moment and looked at Libra. "It's okay. What's the plan now?"

"We get the Dragon's Bit. We get my mother. And then we kill that son of a bitch."

CHAPTER SEVENTEEN

I

The drive to the Incaen Forest was long, and the dark enveloped them all. Kandyce acted as chauffeur in an old wheeler that was on its last legs. It was Libra's vehicle, but she'd insisted on driving. Should the stories be true, she knew, as the fire Etherean, that a lot of what was to happen rested on her. The trial, retrieval of the Dragon's Bit, and who knew what else. She wouldn't be able to sit in the back with the guys and pretend this was a road trip. Her life could soon be on the line. She looked over at Libra sitting silent in the passenger seat. *He must be going through hell, too.*

This made things complicated. When she first got the book on their adventure in the Grand Library, she thought perhaps she could find this artifact and use it for revenge against Talon. Now, this wasn't all just about her. Libra's mother was a hostage. Every time Kandyce thought about it, she felt her temperature rise. Talon had gotten a step ahead of them, and now she had no choice but to hand it over. She wouldn't be able to live with herself if someone else had to go what she went through in losing a loved one to Talon.

She had just driven beyond the city limits into open land. Tall amber lights lit the road every few feet and a large field of grass could barely be seen beyond it. Their ETA was about forty minutes. After a while, her own thoughts settled down, and complaints from Vinzant pulled her into the conversation going on behind her.

"Are we there yet?" Vinzant asked.

"Are you serious?" she responded.

"Jack's taking up all the leg room. It's cramped back here."

Micks shrugged. "I don't mind."

Vinzant rolled his eyes. "Oh, God. Why don't you two just get a room already?"

"Get a what?" said Jack. "Why?"

"You're obviously in love with each other. Just do it and get on with life."

Micks smiled. "Well, if you insist."

Jack waved his hands in protest. "Whoa, whoa, hold up! Me and Micks? Really?"

"What's so wrong with that?" asked Micks.

"How about 'I only like women'?"

"Really?" asked Micks, surprised.

"Yeah. Really. Why? Did I give you a different impression?"

"No, it's just... Yeah, I guess so."

The car went silent. Kandyce just rolled her eyes. She'd been there before. She felt so lucky to have found Mira. The thought was quickly dashed with a heavy shake to the car that rattled them all. She shared a worried glance with Libra as the whistling sound of air escaping a tire rang out. "Shit."

She pulled over and everyone got out to assess the damage. The front tire was flat.

"Great," said Libra.

"Dammit, Libra," she said. "I'm so sorry. Do you have a spare?"

He shook his head. "No. How far away are we?"

"I think about ten minutes, driving distance. But now, probably about an hour if we walk."

Libra sighed. "Guess we'll have to walk. Just get your gear ready. The lusae are out here."

***

The word shook Vinzant to his core. Lusae. He grew stiff, and his eyes only saw the memory playing in his head: On the other side of a wheeler, from under the small space left between its bottom and the ground, he remembered the corpses of a man and a woman by the side of the road.

"You're not scared of a little animal are you, Vinzant?" teased Jack.

Vinzant's mind snapped back to the present. "Are you kidding? Lusae aren't animals. They're magical monsters. We don't stand a chance."

Jack laughed. "Who says?"

"How about my parents?"

The laughter stopped, and Vinzant saw the group grow curious. "The lusae killed them right in front of me."

"I'm sorry to hear that, Vinzant," said Libra. "But, regardless, we have to go anyway. Lusae or not, we've got your back."

Vinzant took a deep breath and followed the group as they walked off into the night.

II

Walking around in the wilderness at night wasn't as bad as Vinzant thought it would be. Kandyce led the way, with a bright, conjured flame in her hand illuminating a small piece of grassland. Vinzant stayed in the middle of the group, shielded by Libra, Jack, and Micks. The paranoia he felt began to subside until Kandyce made a sudden stop.

"What? What is it?" Vinzant asked.

She put a finger to her lips. "Shh."

Vinzant didn't like this. What had she seen or heard? Just as he got a handle on his rising panic, he heard a low growl and the shuffling of feet. His pulse quickened and he looked at Jack and Micks to see if they were playing a trick. They both looked back just as alarmed as he was. He closed his eyes and took a deep breath through his nose but heard another low growl. This time, it was on the opposite side. Okay, he thought, so it just moved. It's just one. Five of us, one of them.

The shuffling sound against the ground grew louder. He heard multiple growls simultaneously.

Whatever they were, they were standing just outside of the radius of Kandyce's light. Vinzant froze with fear.

Libra spoke up in a low, whispery voice, "All right. Looks like we have a fight on our hands. Everyone just stay calm and stay ready. Protect Kandyce. We need to be able to see. You got that?"

"Right," said Jack and Micks.

"Vinzant? Vinzant?"

Vinzant heard Libra, but couldn't find the strength to move. And when the creatures stepped into the light, all five of them, he became that abandoned child by the side of the road all over again. They looked like overgrown dogs with wild black fur and white eyes with no pupils. Sharp white fangs were on full display when they snarled. As soon as one of them jumped into action, all hell broke loose.

Libra defended against one of the dogs and jumped in front of Vinzant to defend him as well. "Wake up, Vinzant!"

"We're dead. You don't know what they can do," Vinzant replied.

"They're wild dogs. Cut 'em down."

"Dammit!" yelled Jack on the opposite side. "I can't move."

Vinzant looked and saw that Jack's right side had been covered in mud. A pillar of hardened dirt connected his raised arm to the ground. He was mid-swing, but unable to complete it in his bound position. Even his feet were covered in mud and stuck to the ground. Vinzant could see that the once solid ground on which they stood had become loose and muddy. He saw that his own feet had sunk an inch and immediately stepped out. "See? This is what they do, Libra. They're not just dogs. They're hockers. They use the earth to trap you and when you can't move, you become their food."

"Well, then we'll just have to not get stuck," said Libra.

"We're on their turf! Anywhere we step could be it —"

"Enough, Vinzant! We need you. It's do or die." Libra called out to the group, "They're earth type! Keep moving your feet and don't get stuck."

"A little late for that," Jack said.

Micks stepped in front of the lunging hocker and defended with his sword. After kicking it back, he swung his blade at the pillar of dirt and set Jack's arm free.

"You okay?" asked Micks.

"Yeah, thanks," said Jack.

"Be careful, Jack."

Seeing everyone fight these things off forced Vinzant to muster up some strength. He didn't want another situation like what had happened to his parents all those years ago. If there was anything he could do, he would push through his fear and do it now. He spotted Kandyce, who seemed to grow tired of simply using her power as a torch. She raised her arm to throw a fireball at her attacker, Vinzant jumped in to fend it off. "No, Kandyce. We got this. Just keep us in the light."

Kandyce increased the radius of light, and Vinzant fought along with the rest of them. He dodged motes of mud kicked up by the hockers and went in for the biggest one, the alpha, the leader of

140

the pack. Vinzant's sword bounced back when the hocker, now covered in mud, hardened his coat in defense. "Oh, come on," he said.

The hocker Vinzant was fighting howled, and all the hockers stopped and stepped back. The battle had a moment of confused calm. In an almost synchronized manner, the hockers stood on their hind legs and plopped back down on their forelegs, causing the puddle of mud to rise and cover each and every one of their prey. Vinzant did his best to dodge the mud, but it was no use. They were all covered in dirt, and it hardened, binding all five of them like statues.

This is it, he thought. From the shoulders down, everyone's body was solid. The mud continued to run down their faces and their throats were exposed. Vinzant knew this was the spot where hockers always went for the kill. The alpha looked Vinzant in his eyes and bared its teeth. If Vinzant didn't know any better, he'd say it was mocking him, smiling and readying for the kill. Vinzant just closed his eyes, sure that the last thing he'd ever see would be the monster's slow recoil before the pounce.

What Vinzant felt next was unexpected. It wasn't a painful bite at the neck, but rather intense heat. He opened his eyes to see the hockers' attention on something in the distance. Vinzant couldn't make out what they were barking at, but in the next moment he saw a bright orange glow that shot past them all. In a flash, the hockers were in flame. The next moment, their forms disintegrated into shadow, leaving behind only echoes of their pained howls.

The mud loosened and everyone shook off what they could.

"What was that?" asked Libra.

Vinzant shrugged, mouth agape, but turned when Kandyce said, "Look!"

Out of the distance came a man. The flame in his hand blanketed him in an orange glow. Day was slowly beginning to break, but the light was still needed to see. He had a fair, wrinkled face, a bald head, and a long, black beard. He was covered in a large, brown robe that was tied at the waist. "Are you the woman of flame?" he asked.

Kandyce glanced at her team, who all wore blank expressions, and said, "The woman of flame?"

"Yes," he said. "The one who will free the dragon. Are you the woman of flame?"

Vinzant watched as Kandyce chose her words carefully. "I'm a fire Etherean, and we all came to find something pertaining to a dragon, but I'm not sure if I'm who—"

"Yes! It is you. Oh, he will be so proud."

"Who?"

"The fire spirit. Come! I will take you to him."

Libra stepped in between them. "I don't think that's necessary. Thank you for saving us, but we got it from here."

"Do you?" the man asked. "Are you sure you can take on more of the lusae? Sure looked like you needed my help."

Vinzant, relieved, cut the conversation short. "Yes, we'll take all the help we can get. Lead the way, sir."

Libra relented, and off the group went with the strange man who had just saved their lives.

III

"Who are you?" asked Kandyce. The daylight was bright enough that they no longer needed fire to see. So, her ring was refueled with the power she once wielded. They had walked for a short while, but the whole time, she was uneasy about this man. How did he know about her?

"I am The Finder. At least, that is what I once was. But that is what you can call me."

"The Finder? And what do you find?"

"I found you, for instance. But most importantly, I found the location of the fire spirit."

"We did, too—"

"Without the help of some book. I have convened with the fire spirit. Become a... companion of sorts. He knows what I want, and I know what he wants."

She could feel herself getting impatient with this conversation. "So, what does he want?"

"More than anything, he wants a body to inhabit so that he may live in the world as he once did." Kandyce slowed her step with this revelation,

145

but The Finder noticed. "Oh, don't be afraid. That's not why he mentioned your name."

"Then why have I come up at all?"

"Because he knows you're coming. He knows your intent."

"And what do you want?"

The Finder let the question linger as the light of a forest forever engulfed in flame came into view. "It seems we are here."

Kandyce marveled at the sight she had only before seen on monitors. "So, this is the Incaen Forest."

"Come! We must not let him wait."

They traveled down the hill and came to a stop in front of a wall of fire.

"Looks like this is all you, Kandyce," said Libra. "You ready?"

"I didn't come all this way to chicken out." She smirked.

"Just wait," The Finder interjected. "He will speak to you soon enough. Everyone else, stand back. Give them some room."

The group did as told, and Kandyce stood in front of the forest. She called out, "I'm here, fire spirit. Hello?" She waited a few awkward moments and almost began to feel foolish. But then…

"Well, well…" said a raspy voice, "You have finally come."

Kandyce went cold. She looked behind her, searching for the source of the voice, but she knew it was none of her crew. It sounded surrounding, all-encompassing. It sent a chill through her body. "Are you the fire spirit?"

"That I am."

"How did you know I was coming?"

"I know the desires of all who seek me and my power. You have spoken the loudest, but there is another whose desire is just as loud. You want the Dragon's Bit for revenge against the very one for which you are here to get it." The fire spirit laughed. "This is so interesting."

"Can the others hear you?"

"No. Only you can hear me."

"Can I have the Dragon's Bit?"

"Ha! You thought it would be that easy? Anyone who wants power of mine must prove themselves worthy."

That's what Kandyce was afraid of, but her survival instincts kicked in and she knew to never show it. "Okay, let's just get this over with."

"If you can stand the heat, then come on in."

Kandyce stepped closer toward the edge of the forest and reached out her hand to the nearest tree. She drew in a breath of surprise to find that its flame wasn't hot. After a quick glance to her team, who all seemed apprehensive, she stepped further into the forest, ready to take on the trial of the fire spirit.

IV

The fire engulfing the forest dissipated except for the perimeter and the tops of the trees.

"The flame doesn't burn you now," said the fire spirit, "but fail in this challenge, and you will end up burned along with the rest."

Kandyce felt a tightness in her abdomen as she noticed the few human skeletons lying on the ground. "What do I do now?"

"You have thirty minutes to find the Dragon's Bit. The fire above you will fall if you don't find it, and when your time is up, it will take you. Now go!"

Kandyce had not the slightest clue where the Dragon's Bit could be. With the fire gone, the forest was easier to navigate, but it was still a dense gathering of lush greens and dusty browns. If the Dragon's Bit wasn't some outstanding color, it could take her forever to find it. Still, she trekked through grass and fallen leaves. She felt the scratch of branches against her skin. She climbed partway up the side of a tree and surveyed the area. Nothing. She glanced up and saw that the flames were indeed making their descent. After jumping to the ground, she looked in bushes, ran one way and then another, but still found nothing. She felt helpless. And hot. Quite different from when she entered. It was then that she knew without a doubt that the fire tumbling downward was indeed different. It would burn her alive if she didn't figure out something quick.

The thought of burning up led to a thought about what brought her here in the first place. That book from the Grand Library had the same finicky properties as the fire here. When her power was activated, it burned the hand of that woman who had tried to grab it. But it didn't hurt Kandyce. What if the Dragon's Bit had the same properties? She had to give it a shot. The glow from her ring went out as she used her own ether to gather fire in her palm. Perhaps the Dragon's Bit would be activated and burn whatever it was near. She hoped it would be. Beads of sweat began to gather at her brow as the forest's flames fell lower.

"There's not much time left," teased the fire spirit. "It was so much fun getting to know you."

Kandyce tried her best to block out his voice and search for smoke, fire, or any sign that what she did had worked. The flames came down so far, that she had to lower her head to keep from being burned. When she did, she saw a sign. A patch of grass in the distance was alight with flames shooting upward; a strange opposition to the unnatural path of the fire above.

She made a dash for it, but the fire above her got lower and lower. She got closer to the artifact, but had to crawl on her hands and knees. When she was only a few feet away, the fire descended so close that she had to crawl on her stomach. She dragged herself forward with her elbows and knees, all the while feeling the intense heat that singed her back. She had come so close that she just couldn't let it end here. Mira's death would not be in vain. She would have Talon's head, Dragon's Bit or not.

She reached out, just inches away from the patch of burning grass. Mere seconds away from being burned, she grabbed hold of something round and long. It had the texture of a wooden pole. She prayed that would be enough as the fires above finally fell on top of her.

V

While everyone else was sitting, Libra was standing. They were all waiting for Kandyce to re-emerge from the forest, but would she? The sound of the group's laughter after Vinzant cracked a joke bugged him. What could they possibly laugh about right now? One of their friends was in a burning forest by herself. Putting her life on the line for him. For his mother. Couldn't they understand how serious this was? He couldn't hold his tongue. "Could you guys shut up?"

They were all taken aback by the sudden outburst. Vinzant opened his mouth to say something, but was stopped by Jack's hand on his shoulder and a shake of his head.

Libra again faced the forest, blinking, hoping to refresh the static image that lay before him to see Kandyce come walking out.

"You are worried," said The Finder. His voice was in a near whisper and startled Libra, who had all but forgotten he was there. "It is as though you have the most to lose. Yet, you are not in the forest."

"I'm not an Etherean. Doubt I could do much in there."

"Why do you seek the Dragon's Bit?"

Libra got a closer look at the man and saw his round face had more wrinkles than he first noticed, and some of his teeth were missing. There was something behind his eyes — a knowing. It felt like he didn't seek knowledge, but confirmation. Libra wanted to see where this went. "My mother is being held for ransom."

The Finder nodded, broke eye contact, and stood in solidarity next to him. "I see."

To Libra's chagrin, The Finder revealed nothing. So, he pressed, "You didn't answer Kandyce's question earlier."

"Kandyce! Is that her name? And what question was that?"

"What do you want? Why are you helping us?"

"Isn't that what one does when he sees his fellow man in distress?"

"I'm just gonna be frank. I think you have ulterior motives."

"And if I did, telling you would be pointless."

"Try me."

The Finder sighed and smiled. "Do you know of the Servants of Elao? Of course, you don't. It is an old Etherean guild lost to the sands of time. I was a part of it. Our sole purpose was to restore our god, Elao, to power, but I never saw the sense in it. Elao was always in power—still could be, if he wanted it to be so. The legend says that he abdicated his power and left it to watch over us. Abandon us is more like it. Does he not see the pain and suffering of the very people he created?" The Finder clenched his fist and gritted his teeth. "I couldn't stay in that guild with their fanciful notions of appeasing a god who left us to rot. There is another who hasn't left us. One who has been trapped right here along with us for centuries. The one I hope to restore to power and save us all. Calamity."

Libra hadn't realized they'd been hanging around a worshiper of the god of destruction this whole time. He decided not to respond. While what The Finder said terrified him, none of it could possibly come to pass. But here he was, in front of a burning forest, supposedly housing a fire spirit. What was really going on in the world?

Libra was snapped back to his present situation. Flames danced around a human frame that emerged from the forest. When they dissipated, he saw Kandyce and a light at the end of the tunnel for his mother's rescue. When he saw what was in her hand, all at once, his fears stopped eating away at him and he was buoyed by hope. The guys gathered around and shared their praise and relief.

"Did you get it?" Libra asked.

"You tell me," she said, holding her chin up with pride. She held out her hand and revealed what looked to be a small stick of about six inches long. Libra touched it and noticed that, while it looked wooden, the material was a leathery and a bit pliable.

"This is supposed to summon a dragon?"

Kandyce shrugged. "Seems far-fetched. I tried, but I can't figure out how it works. However, I'd be a fool to disbelieve anything right about now."

CHAPTER EIGHTEEN

I

Now that they had the Dragon's Bit, Libra felt a little better. Yet, he couldn't shake himself free from the specter of dread. His mother was still in captivity, and who was to say whether Talon would honor the deal or not? The group would have to be ready for anything. However, right now, the wheeler was still down one tire. Although they made it back to the road safely, making it back home was another dilemma.

Vinzant groaned. "If only the Middle Third would share their hover tech, we wouldn't have to worry about wheels."

Jack's deep voice spoke up. "There's no way we're making it back to town on foot."

"We could call a tow service, but it might take them a couple hours to get out here," said Micks.

"Or, we ask our fellow warriors for help," said Kandyce. "We did pass a few military buildings on the way. They're not too far from here."

Libra could tell that the group was getting restless. As the leader, he made a decision. "That sounds good. Let's grab our stuff and head there."

Vinzant mocked him with a showy salute. "Yes, captain!"

Libra laughed, knowing Vinzant could see through his bullshit. Right then, he was so happy to have Vinzant around. He needed that laugh. And they all needed a break from the tension.

II

They reached the military building within a half hour. The few snacks that they had packed were all eaten on the way, but did little to satiate their hunger. Libra held a hand over his aching stomach as it growled.

Vinzant snorted a laugh. "I feel the same way, too, buddy."

As they approached the large steel doors of the warrior compound, they saw two men standing guard on the outside; one bearded, the other clean-shaven. Their swords were out, pointed to the ground with their hands resting on the hilts. Libra slowed his step at the sight of them. They were stern and silent. Both were dressed in the obsidian armor of the Southern Third's military, and both were burly enough to intimidate the everyday man. Libra made an amused sound, thinking, *I am no everyday man.*

He took a step closer, and that's when they sprang into action. One sword from each of the men was crossed in a scissors-like display blocking the doors. "This area is off-limits," said the bearded guard on the right. "What business do you have here?" inquired the other.

Libra cautiously said, "One at a time, fellas. We came because our car broke down. We're just looking for some help."

One guard eyed the group, specifically their swords and BACs. "Looks like you're trying to barge in to me."

Libra huffed in annoyance, but tried his best to remain polite. "I assure you, sir, we are only here for assistance."

The guards exchanged a glance and lowered their swords. "Remove your arms. Place them over there," one of the guards instructed, gesturing to the side of where the group stood. Everyone complied, and the bearded guard stayed put while the clean-shaven guard opened the door and led the way inside.

The complex was expansive with multiple buildings spread throughout and bordered by a large concrete wall. Warriors populated the entire area; men and women were dressed in their black stretchy workout gear, some were in plainclothes, and only a few were in full battle gear like the group's guide. "We'll find somebody to help you," he said. They walked some more, and he told them of the different buildings: the men's and women's barracks, the training ground at the center, the mess hall, and recruiting. It wasn't a huge complex by any stretch of imagination, but it certainly wasn't small. None of them had expected to see so much hiding in plain sight, just off the road.

They slowed when they reached the training ground at the center. A well-built man with dark hair sat on the metal bleachers, watching the practice happening in front of him intently. He puffed out a cloud of cigarette smoke as Libra's guide called to him, "Hey! Locke."

The man turned his head slowly, revealing a bit gray hair in the front. Locke's eyes revealed a look of annoyance. "What is it?"

"Think you can help these guys out? They need some food and a tire change."

"You want me to babysit?"

"Unless you want to be on door duty…"

With only a puff of air, Locke dropped his argument and accepted what he was being asked to do.

The guide went back to his post at the door.

Libra sensed that they were being a bother and offered, "Hey, we can find someone else if—"

"No, you're all right," said Locke. "'A warrior's duty is to his people,' and all that…"

***

The food was just okay, normal fare for warriors, nothing fancy. They ate it all the same. When they were done, Locke took them back to their car to replace the tire with one they had at their compound. All five of them stood around waiting for Locke to finish his duty as a warrior. He refused to let them handle it themselves, citing a code of honor. "No, I'll handle it," he said.

"We really thank you for doing this, man," said Vinzant. "Our guy, Libra, needs to get back home ASAP."

Locke tightened the last lug nut with a raised brow. "What's the rush?"

"His mom is—" Vinzant stopped, feeling Kandyce's hand on his shoulder.

Locke stood up with the wrench in his hand and softened his expression. It was obvious he could sense the seriousness of the situation. "It's like that, huh? Well, you don't have to tell me, but I hope you pull through, and your mom," he directed at Libra.

"Thanks," Libra responded.

"You need any of us for backup?"

Libra smirked. "We're good. It's almost over now. And we can take care of ourselves."

Locke eyed their gear and gave half a smile. "Yeah, I'd say so. You guys take care."

Once he got in his car, closed the door, and drove off, Micks couldn't stop looking in the vehicle's direction. "Who *was* that?"

Vinzant, ever ready for the chance to make light of a situation, noticed Micks' interest. He wrapped his arm around Micks and said, "That, my man, is who we call one of the good guys."

"He's everything."

"Hey! What's he got that I don't got?"

Micks jerked his head, looked in Vinzant's eyes, down to his feet, and back to his eyes again. He removed the arm from his shoulders, and his only answer was a hearty laugh.

Kandyce chimed in. "What he's got is 'body'. Something you'd know about if you worked out once in a while." This got the whole group laughing while Vinzant nodded in appreciation of a good roast. The over-the-top laughter showed him they had all been waiting to turn the tables on him for some time.

Micks opened the back passenger side door of the wheeler with his giggles subsiding. "Come on, Auctorats, we have a mother to save."

They all followed suit, with Vinzant lagging behind, the last one to get in. "Auctorats? New team name?"

"Auctori?" said Jack, fishing for the correct term.

"Auctorati," said Libra from the front seat.

A noticeable hush came over them. Vinzant broke the silence, of course, while closing the door behind him. "Has a nice ring to it!"

CHAPTER NINETEEN

The whole drive home, all Kandyce could think of was Mira. She had died at the hands of Talon's thugs, and now, with the Dragon's Bit in her possession, Kandyce had leverage over the man she wanted dead. *But Libra's mother...* she thought, cutting her eye to him in the passenger seat. She turned her attention back to the road and tried to push the thoughts from her mind, but they kept creeping back. She should take the Bit, summon the dragon, and burn Talon's house down with him inside. But that wouldn't work. She had already tried using the artifact once. There must have been something she had done wrong. Regardless, she thought of Libra's mother and wondered, if she were in his shoes, what would she want to happen? Nobody else should have to die at the hands of Talon. And although her plans had changed, her mission remained the same. She'd just have to take him out before he used the Dragon's Bit. As soon as Talon handed over Libra's mother, he was a dead man.

***

Micks wasn't asleep, but he pretended to be, cradled in the nook of a sleeping Jack's arm. He hadn't felt so at peace since...well, since he could even remember. His family had abandoned him when they found out about his illegal dealings. They weren't wealthy, but Micks always knew he deserved more. He wanted to live like the nobles in the Middle Third. The best of the best. His family would say that as long they had each other, they lived well. But he saw it as settling for a lifestyle of scraping from one check to the next. He found a contact in the criminal underworld, figuring one job would be enough, and it was. He made a large enough reward to support himself and live slightly better than his own family did. But then he met a man, fell in love, and was robbed of everything. After fighting the feeling of defeat, Micks settled it in his mind that he lost everything because he had become complacent. His heart got in the way; he wouldn't make that mistake again.

Still, snuggling against Jack's hard body, Micks had to admit that it was tempting to let it all go. Life could be so much easier if he just accepted where he was right now. But he reminded himself that Jack didn't—couldn't—love him the way he wanted. And that "right now" was as much a dream as the future he desired. So, which was more tangible, more possible? Certainly not a life with Jack. And he wouldn't dare go groveling back to his family. He only had one other option, and that was to take his money and run.

He could have done that sooner. Libra and the gang never had to see him again after his mother was kidnapped. Micks had the money he was promised, and it was enough to start a life in the Middle Third. But, he wouldn't be living like a noble.

168

He came on this trip, half out of guilt for Libra's predicament, but also to see if they could indeed get the artifact he wanted so badly. Now that they had it, he could get the funds he needed from Talon to make his dreams a reality. One last betrayal, he thought to himself. He soaked in all the fake love from Jack while he could, because in a moment, they would all hate him.

CHAPTER TWENTY

I

All Libra could think about when they got back was getting his mother home safely. Night had fallen, and the team was understandably tired, especially Kandyce. They all decided to crash at the warehouse. Libra held open the large overhead sliding door, allowing each of his team to step in. Kandyce was the last to walk through, and he pulled her aside. He looked into her eyes with wonder at the woman who seemed to come from out of nowhere, but was so necessary right now. "Where would I be without you?" he said.

Kandyce blushed. "Libra, please…"

"No, really. If it wasn't for you, I wouldn't have a chance at getting my mother back. I'm just so grateful. You don't even know."

Kandyce laid a hand on his shoulder and gave him a kind expression. "You're welcome. Tomorrow, we get that bastard and your mom." She patted him on the side of the arm and turned to her part of the warehouse.

Watching her walk away, Libra felt so happy and grateful, he could have kissed her. Kandyce was not his to have, however, and he knew he'd probably get slugged in the face for such a gesture. For now, the only woman he needed to focus on was being held captive. *But not for long*, he thought. He was ready to bring her home.

Micks surprised Libra from behind and killed his train of thought. "Hey," Micks said. "You ready to do this tomorrow?"

Libra opened his palm and looked at the coveted Dragon's Bit in his hand. "Yeah."

"You're not just gonna hand it over, are you?"

"What other choice do I have?"

Vinzant's voice called out from a corner of the room. "What? No, Libra. We have what he wants. Now you get what you want."

"Well, of course I'll make sure my mom's safe first—"

"But not only safe," said Kandyce. "In our protection. He has to hand her over first."

"And then we make him sorry he ever laid a hand on her," said Jack. "He's not getting that Bit."

Libra marveled at group he had gathered around him. Their faces were eager and determined. He knew then that it was not only about him and his mother, but about all of them. He couldn't give Talon any more power. He needed to end this. They all did.

"You know," said Libra, "he'll probably have a lot of bodyguards around him. He's not letting us out without a fight."

"Then we fight," said Micks.

Libra smiled. "Yeah. We fight."

Kandyce and Jack smiled at Libra while Vinzant punched the palm of his own hand, exclaiming, "Whoo! Cracking skulls time!"

After a chuckle, they all started to break off for bed.

"Goodnight, Libra," said Micks.

Libra went to his own space and gently rubbed the Dragon's Bit between his fingers. He didn't know how he would sleep. He felt charged, ready for action, ready to get his mother back, and ready to fight Talon. As he slipped the Bit into a bag he had hanging on the wall, he could have sworn he felt eyes on him. He spun around, but all he saw was Micks heading to his own bed. That old nagging suspicion reared up in the back of Libra's mind, but he shooed it away. Micks had only been a help this whole time. Libra knew he had nothing to worry about.

II

Micks was awake just before daybreak. Everyone else was asleep. He looked at Jack, whom he'd slept next to the night before, and let out a sigh that signified the end of their friendship. He glanced at Libra, but found he couldn't hold his eyes on him for too long. The guilt of what he planned to do had begun to creep in. He had to cut it off before he changed his mind. *Leave your heart out of this*, he reminded himself.

He slid his hand into Libra's bag that was hanging on the wall. It was where he'd seen Libra place the Dragon's Bit the night before. He felt the smooth, leathery texture against his fingers and pulled it out. *Got it.*

A glance at the Dragon's Bit in his hand led him to wonder how crazy it would be to have a dragon at his beck-and-call. When he thought about it last night, he pondered possibly selling it. That idea fell to the wayside, for he figured he hadn't enough time to find another buyer before having Libra come after him. Talon was the only choice. It was time for

174

Micks to collect his money and get out of this god-forsaken city.

CHAPTER TWENTY-ONE

I

There was no slow awakening for Libra. The urgency of the day caused him to become fully awake with the first signal to his brain. He looked around and saw Jack, Vinzant, and Kandyce already up and geared as they enjoyed a bit of breakfast. His heart warmed at the sight, and he was so grateful to feel supported with such a heavy burden.

"Hey, sleepyhead," called Vinzant.

"Hey guys," Libra said, smiling. He noticed the amused reactions on his team's faces and knew he was smiling too much. He tried his best to reel it in.

"You ready?" said Kandyce.

"Yeah. Are you guys ready?"

Jack nodded. "We're gonna bring her home."

Libra glanced to his left, then to his right. Someone was missing. "Where's Micks?" They all shared a look to see if anyone had any idea, but no answer came. Libra tried to fight the paranoid turning in his stomach. "Was he here when you woke up?"

Jack shrugged and shook his head. "No."

Micks repeatedly leaving the group without a word, having no background that the Enforcers could check, setting Jack up for murder; for Libra, all of the suspicions that Micks couldn't be trusted came flooding back. Libra yanked his bag off the wall and dumped the contents on the ground. Libra made a deep groan, shook his head, and rubbed his temples with a thumb and forefinger.

Kandyce asked, "Libra, what's wrong?"

"The Dragon's Bit's gone."

"What?" she replied, aghast. "You think Micks took it?"

Libra covered his face then ran both hands to the back of his skull, revealing a reddened face. "Shit. Shit!"

"Wait a minute," Jack protested. "He wouldn't do that."

"Yes, he would. He's fucking shifty, Jack."

"No, Libra. He—"

"He ruined your life!"

Jack looked at Libra, puzzled.

"He set you up to take the fall for the mayor. He was hired to kill him, and then he set you up. He told me himself. How else would he know beyond a shadow of a doubt that you were innocent?"

The room fell silent. Jack moved his lips to say something, but the words wouldn't come.

Libra continued, "How long have you all been awake?"

"About an hour, hour and a half," said Kandyce.

"He's been gone at least that long and hasn't come back… Gone with the Dragon's Bit."

"Damn…" said Vinzant. "We gotta find him."

Libra seethed. "I think I know where he went."

II

Micks was surprised to see the mayor at Talon's estate when he was let in.

The mayor glared at him from his wheelchair and asked, "Is this the one who was responsible, Talon?"

Talon turned from the window and caught Micks's gaze. "Yes, I'm certain of it. He set up the chef to look like your attacker, but it was really him all along."

Micks felt his heart skip a beat and his stomach pulse with worry. Was this an ambush? "What are you talking about?"

"Please, Micks. Did you really think I wouldn't have you followed? All of the evidence was in your ratty apartment. I even found that you infiltrated my gang. You caused me to lose the book I was after."

Micks's body temperature rose, but he tried to keep calm. "So? I was hired to do all that. It was nothing personal. And we have a deal now, anyway.

I'm holding up my end of the bargain." He held out the Dragon's Bit in his palm.

"Give me that," said Talon, reaching out.

Micks snatched it back. "The money first."

"After what you pulled? You're lucky I don't strike you down right now."

"Give me my money, or I will call down the dragon myself."

Talon folded his hands behind his back and grinned. "Do it."

Micks started to breathe hard. He was in over his head. Talon was calling his bluff, and all he could think to do was wave the stick around and hope this would scare him. His cheeks felt flushed when both Talon and Mayor Wilhelm began laughing. And the next moment, he was on the ground with the Dragon's Bit being ripped from his fingers and his face being shoved away. Talon treated him like a playground bully.

"It's finally mine," marveled Talon. "That was a nice try, Micks, but you literally don't have what it takes to make this work."

"And what is that?"

Talon held the Bit in his metal hand and the tips of his fingers glowed red.

Micks's eyes grew wide as did the mayor's.

Mayor Wilhelm tried to speak. "You're…"

"A fire Etherean. Surprise." Talon raised the artifact and its two ends extended a few feet. "A lost legend, found in a rare book that was held only in the library of Lorelei Castle, tells us that, to summon a dragon, one must have power over fire and speak its name. You see, there are, in fact, three books, and this was the second. At its spine was the apex and base of the triangle you thought complete with only the first and third books you retrieved. It recorded the name of the only dragon in history to be controlled by man. Ekkhard!" he called.

A shockwave originating from the Bit shook the house and shattered the nearest windows. Micks felt nauseated. He knew he was about to come face to face with a dragon.

CHAPTER TWENTY-TWO

I

The drive to Talon's estate was excruciating for Libra. He only had his mother in mind and a blinding rage at Micks, who had double-crossed him. He whipped and bounced through the streets, and even though it was early morning, the few cars that were in the road felt like huge obstacles. He had forgotten all about the passengers he'd been traveling with: Kandyce, Jack, and Vinzant.

The earth shook as a violent boom echoed in the skies like thunder.

"What was that?" asked Vinzant.

"I don't know," said Kandyce. "Whatever it was wasn't natural. You don't think it was the Dragon's Bit, do you, Libra?"

He gave no response. He was barely aware that the others were speaking.

Crossing one of the outer streets of the city into Lotus Valley was like changing from night to day. The dirty, dusty view of the city suddenly became clean sidewalks, green grass, and trees. Talon's estate slowly came into view.

It was guarded by a wrought-iron gate and protected by mercenaries.

Libra hit the gas.

"Libra," Kandyce warned.

"Hold on tight, guys."

The mercs at the gate scattered, and Libra's wheeler rammed straight through. After traversing the open grounds, he slammed the brakes at the sight of a small army that was blocking the way through to the front door.

Libra looked back at his team. "This is it."

II

Micks was still on the ground, cautious as Talon approached and towered over him.

"Now, tell me," said Talon, "who hired you to kill me?"

Micks hesitated, trying to figure out if that one secret was the last thing keeping him alive.

His strategizing was interrupted by a sudden burst through the door. A rush of mercenaries came in, swords and BACs drawn. "The Auctorat," said one. "He's here!"

Talon smiled. "Let him in. And bring down our guest."

III

The battle on the expansive front lawn was getting on Libra's nerves. They'd only been fighting for five minutes, but it felt like they were getting no closer to the front door.

"Are you all powered up yet, Kandyce?" he asked, fending off another attack.

Kandyce took a glance at her ring. "Almost, just a few more seconds."

Libra saw her ring brighten up and glow red. It was time to scorch all of them.

Just as Kandyce enveloped her arm in flame, several of the mercenaries began to back down.

Vinzant smirked. "All it takes is a little fire, and these guys fold."

"It's not that," said Libra, dropping his guard. He could see they were all listening to something. A radio?

One of the mercs stepped forward and said, "You can go in, Libra."

Libra's stomach tightened, and he shared a few worried glances with his team. It was too easy.

But he didn't have a choice. Until then, he'd forgotten they all knew who he was. He removed the bandana from his face. Screw his identity. If his mother was inside, she was all that mattered.

***

Micks watched as a sickly blonde-haired woman in her nightgown was brought in. He gathered that she must be Libra's mother and feared where this was going.

"Take her to the window," Talon ordered. He turned to Micks. "Who hired you? Tell me or your friend loses his mother. Do you really want her blood on your hands?"

Micks shot a look behind him at the ever-increasing volume of footsteps. His face grew hot with shame as he saw his team approaching.

***

Libra caught eye contact with the traitor and charged. "Micks! You son of a—" he stopped in his tracks, taking in the full scene. "Mom!" He withdrew his sword and pointed it at Talon's neck. "Let her go."

Talon smirked and swatted the weapon away like a fly. "Hello Auctorat. I was just having a talk with your friend here. I'll spare your mother if he tells me who hired him."

Micks shook his head, "I can't, Libra. As soon as I say it, he'll kill us all."

"You don't have a choice," said Libra. He turned his sword to the traitor. "If anything happens to my mother, I'll kill you myself. Tell him what you know."

Micks stood up and swallowed hard. "It was a Mr. Draw. One of your rivals in the crystal business."

"Hmph," said Talon. "I'll deal with him later. Honestly, I was hoping you'd say Mayor Wilhelm. That would have given me a more justifiable reason to kill him. As it stands, you will all have to deal with the fact that there's no room for a mayor in this city anymore."

Talon walked over to Wilhelm, causing him to shrink back. "Kill me? Talon, I—"

"I'll make this quick and painless." With a quick swipe of Talon's extended claws, Wilhelm was covered in his own blood from the neck down. "Get rid of her," he called to the men holding Libra's mother. "We're done here."

"No!" yelled Libra. He ran toward the third-floor window, his adrenaline making every second seem to pass in slow motion. He was nearly unaware of Kandyce, Jack, and Vinzant fighting off the mercs that tried to stop him. All he could see was the look of fear in his mother's eyes as she reached out to him. It would be a look he'd never forget. It couldn't end this way. Her body flipped out of the window and into the open air. Libra almost lost his balance at the edge, but caught her hand just in time.

"Hold on, Mom! Just hold on!" He knew she was too weak. Her hand started to slip until only their fingertips touched. Libra looked around frantically for a piece of rope or anything that his mother could grasp, but saw there was nothing. "Mom…"

"Grab my hand!" yelled Micks. He'd just run to Libra's side and stuck his arm downward.

Libra's mother reached up, and Micks got a better grip around her wrist. Together, Libra and Micks pulled her to safety.

Libra hugged his mother tightly. "I'm so sorry I got you into this." Just as his heart began to calm down, what sounded like a loud, squawking roar filled the air from outside.

"It would seem my ride is here," Talon announced.

Libra watched as Talon stood still. All went silent, then a boom rocked the whole house as large red claws came crashing through the wall. Libra shielded his mother from the debris. When he looked back, his skin went cold at the sight of the creature. If its red scales, yellow eyes, and razor-sharp teeth weren't enough, it had a long snout that seemed to distort the air around it with each breath, like gas on a stove.

Talon climbed atop the dragon, hooking the Dragon's Bit in its mouth and holding the reins in his hands. "Kill them," he ordered his men. "It was nice knowing you, Auctorat."

The dragon took a step back, ready for flight.

Libra watched as Kandyce went running. "Oh, no you don't!" She jumped and kicked Talon off the dragon. He fell through the hole in the wall and down three stories to the ground.

CHAPTER TWENTY-THREE

I

Kandyce could see the fight was not over yet. After kicking Talon through the gaping hole in the wall, the dragon leapt after him and caught him on his wing. Kandyce took advantage of the silent, stunned state of the room and started to run downstairs as quickly as she could.

"Where are you going?" asked Vinzant.

"To finish this."

"We're going with you," said Jack.

"Come on, then," she replied. "Libra?"

Libra hoisted his mother up and shook his head. "No. I'm going to the car. I can't leave her."

"I'll go with him," said Micks.

Kandyce was wary of Micks's sudden support but knew Libra could handle himself.

Before leaving, she watched Jack move to Micks and grab him by the front of his shirt. "You set me up! It was you this whole time. I hope it was worth it, you son of a bitch. You're worse than Talon. At least he owns who he is."

"Jack," urged Kandyce. They had no time. They couldn't let Talon escape.

Jack threw Micks back to the ground and turned to Kandyce. "Let's go."

With Vinzant and Jack following behind, she traversed the stairwell, opened the front door, and was greeted by the dragon on the front lawn. Talon stood beside it.

"I figured my takeover can wait a few minutes," he said. "It seems you have something to get off your chest."

Kandyce drew her sword. "There's nothing left to say, Talon. I've been waiting a long time for this. It's time to put you down!"

Talon laughed and rolled his eyes. "Okay. Ekkhard! Burn them."

As the dragon drew in a large breath, she could sense Jack and Vinzant's trepidation. She'd have to think of something fast. Soon she'd feel the intense heat of a continuous line of flame spit out by the dragon. She held up her hands, the dragon opened its mouth, and in a split-second everything was red.

She was surprised at first, then relieved to see that what she'd done was working. She manipulated the fire as it came out, creating what looked like a spherical force field that caused the flames to shoot out around her in every direction. Jack and Vinzant stayed close, clear of the dragon's attack, but were still incredibly hot and sweaty because of it.

"Uh, Kandyce?" warned Vinzant.

Once the dragon spit the last of his flames, Kandyce turned to see what Vinzant was talking about. Talon's estate, the house that Libra, his mother, and Micks were in, was burning down.

II

First, there was a sudden spike in temperature. Libra thought this strange, but only discerned they were in danger when he smelled smoke. Talon's remaining henchmen started scrambling away.

Micks looked into the hallway and jogged back in. "Libra, we gotta move quicker than this."

Libra glared at Micks. "I know that."

"Well, come on then."

Libra lifted his mother to her feet and shouldered most of her weight. Micks went to Libra's opposite side to help hold his mother up, but stopped when Libra said, "Don't you dare fucking touch her."

"Libra. You have to know, I never meant for any of this to happen. I never wanted you or your mother to get hurt."

"Whether you did or not, you betrayed me. And my mother had to pay the price. Don't ask for forgiveness. You're not getting it."

"Boys!" she said, coughing. "Burning house. Focus. I don't need to be carried. I can walk just fine."

195

"But can you run?" asked Libra.

"Well," she smiled, "if running is needed, then you can help me." She coughed again; the smoke was getting thicker. "Let's just get out of here."

The three of them left through the hallway. Libra handed his mother his black handkerchief and gestured for her to cover her mouth as they went down the large staircase to the second floor. They quickly turned the corner, but Libra reared back, seeing the steps to the first floor covered in flame. "Dammit."

"This way," said Micks.

They followed Micks to a large balcony at the back of the house. Libra looked over the edge. It was almost a fifteen-foot drop to the ground.

Libra frowned at Micks. "You want us to jump all the way down?"

Micks waved his arms in a loose shrug. "We have no choice."

Libra looked at his mother. He felt lost. How in the world would she make it? "Mom…"

"Don't think, Libra. We'll find a way."

Micks turned from Libra and looked over the balcony. "Maybe we can use the pillars. I'll go first."

He went to the far corner, where the pillar held up the balcony, and stepped over the low iron rail. After maneuvering himself into position, he dropped and hung to the small slab of the balcony floor with his fingertips. From there, he let go and quickly wrapped his arms around the pillar.

Libra watched as he deftly slid down a few feet and pushed off, making a daring landing on the ground. Micks beckoned them to come down.

"Come on, Mom—"

"Libra…"

Libra turned to see what was wrong. She had tried her best to be strong this whole time, but he finally saw the fear in her eyes.

"I can't," she said.

"Mom, don't say that." His voice cracked, and he could barely keep his tears at bay. "We're getting out of here." Libra jerked his head back toward Micks when he heard his name being called.

"Libra! I can catch her!" Micks yelled.

"What! That's crazy."

"I got her. I know I've lost it, but you need to trust me just this last time."

Libra looked back to the house. A wall of flame obstructed the view inside. This really was the only way. He looked at his mother. She began shaking her head in protest. "Be strong, Mom." He scooped her up in his arms and launched her at Micks. She went screaming all the way down.

III

"A fellow fire Etherean!" said Talon. "Now I see how you were able to find the Dragon's Bit in the first place."

Kandyce wasted no time talking and launched her assault. With her sword drawn, she ran at Talon, launching two darts of fire from her palm. He easily dismissed these with a wave of his hand, but it gave her enough time to close in and strike. He blocked with his metallic arm and countered with a punch to her side.

Vinzant and Jack attacked Talon from either side, but with a kick to Vinzant's gut and Ekkhard's growl and threatening stare at Jack, he warded them off.

Talon laughed at his new pet's loyalty. "Down, boy. I can take care of these hooligans myself."

IV

Micks felt a sharp pain in his abdomen and his left arm. Breathing came hard and it was as if he were breathing through a straw. For a moment, he'd forgotten what had transpired, but when he felt a smooth hand on his face and saw the worried look of Libra's mother, he quickly remembered. "You're, you're alive..." he said. Each word was a struggle.

"Yes, yes. Just breathe. Calm down. You're okay. Breathe."

He did his best, and slowly but surely, his lungs found their rhythm again.

"Mom!" called Libra. He'd landed safely and rushed over. "Oh, thank God." He knelt down to embrace her and caught eye contact with Micks. "Thank you."

Micks tried to straighten up, but he yelled in pain.

"Lie still," said Libra.

"I can't... I can't move my arm. It hurts. And I think I broke a rib."

"Just, stay still. You're gonna be okay." Libra stood.

"Where are you going?" his mother asked.

"To finish this. You stay here with Micks. Don't move." He ran around toward the front of the house and disappeared from view.

Despite having caught Libra's mother, Micks knew he could never really make up for what he did. That hurt more than anything. He had the money now, though. It wasn't as much as he'd hoped for, but it would be enough to live comfortably in Reor. He'd make sure Libra's mother was safe, but it was time to cut his losses.

V

Libra rounded the corner to the front of the house and saw Kandyce, Vinzant, and Jack trying their best to take down Talon. He charged in swinging. "Talon!"

Talon saw Libra coming and threw a ball of fire at Vinzant that hit him in the chest. Vinzant backed off and rolled to the ground, trying to extinguish the flame. Jack followed after him to help. Kandyce was undeterred and continued swinging. Libra came in with his own strikes.

Talon blocked, dodged, and swung, getting in plenty of hits. "Is that all, Auctorat? Savior of the city? Probuston belongs to me."

Libra fell back after a clean punch to his jaw.

Talon punched Kandyce in the gut, grabbed her by the neck, and slammed her to the ground. "You will all kneel to me! You, my brother, the Queen—everyone! I've worked hard for everyone's approval all my life, but do I get any appreciation? No! This is my time! And you're not taking it away from me!"

Libra saw Jack and Vinzant from the corner of his eye. Vinzant's shirt was off, burned and discarded, and he slowly reached for the BAC slung around his back. Jack crept slowly behind Talon. The dragon noticed. It snorted and huffed, trying to get its master's attention. Libra shared a knowing glance with Kandyce and did his best to keep Talon unaware.

"You're wrong, Talon. You don't get appreciated for taking from people. Your time is up."

Talon's smug expression went blank as he felt Jack's large arms wrap around his waist. His legs went flying into the air as Jack suplexed him, causing his neck and back to hit the ground hard.

Libra and Kandyce jumped at the opportunity. Just as Jack moved away, Libra drove his sword through Talon's hand while Kandyce pinned his prosthetic arm to ground with a stab at the wrist. Vinzant trained his gun to Talon's head, but hesitated when he saw Kandyce raise her hand.

Fire leapt from the burning house behind Kandyce and swirled around her hand. She created a flaming spear, but there was so much fire that its end stretched almost twenty feet in the air. "This is for Mira, you bastard!" She drove the point straight through Talon's chest.

Libra watched and listened to the man's cries as he burned from the inside out. In the future, he would look back at this moment, surprised at his feelings. What would have been revulsion only weeks ago was now satisfaction.

Libra jumped when dragon roared at them all. Kandyce paid the dragon no mind. She held onto the fiery spike with fury in her eyes.

Libra cautiously touched her elbow. "Kandyce. The dragon."

She snapped out of it just in time to dodge the dragon's snapping jaws.

They all readied themselves for a fight with the dragon, but saw that it only wanted to protect its master. Ekkhard drew in the spike of flame with a breath and gently grabbed Talon's corpse, looping a tooth through a piece of his armor. It yanked and tossed Talon into the sky like a rag doll.

They all covered their faces from the hard gust of wind that picked up as the dragon took off. It caught Talon's body on its back and flew away.

CHAPTER TWENTY-FOUR

I

L ibra sat down next to his mother on the couch in their living room. Even though the sun was shining through the windows, dark clouds were all that Libra felt in his heart. It had been a week since what had transpired with Talon, and the smoke inhalation seemed to push his mother over the edge. He wrapped an arm around her shoulders and held her hand. They sat in silence for a moment, knowing the end was near.

The monitor across the room was a welcomed distraction. It showed footage of the induction of a new mayor. She was hand-picked by the Southern Third's commander. After the news of Talon's plan spread, along with the tale of how he assassinated the previous mayor, it was said that the commander wanted to pick someone who would work tirelessly to turn the city around. Mayor Alaya Winters was about to make a speech, and Libra watched closely to see if she was indeed the turning point he'd fought for.

"Commander Azure, people of Probuston, I thank you for the honor of being your new mayor. I know this is an unusual moment in our history, but I assure you that we will turn this city around. By now, I'm sure plenty of you have heard of Talon, his crimes against the city, the dragon threat he brought to our doorstep, and the murder of Mayor Wilhelm.

"Up to now, our Enforcers have been working to find the vigilantes responsible for Talon's supposed death. But I, for one, am quite grateful for their service to this city. And so, I hereby close the investigation into the search for Talon's body and the people involved. I ask that, whoever they are, they continue working within the confines of the law to help bring down the crime of this city. I ask that law enforcement recognize them as bounty hunters and create a solution to work together. I also propose an end to the Crystal Tax to help relieve the strain on our economy.

"We've faced hard moments in Probuston, and many of them will end, but it's going to take hard work from all of us. I have faith that, with time, we can restore Probuston to its former glory."

Libra felt his mother stir. She looked up at him and smiled. "You did it, Libra. I'm so proud of you. You have to keep going."

"Keep going? After everything I put you through?"

"This is progress. You have to fight to keep the strides you've made." She laid her head back down. "Besides, we both know there's not much time left. You won't have me to worry about."

"Mom, don't say that."

"I've made my peace. I'm just happy to know that the world is in good hands with you."

Libra squeezed his mother and a tear rolled down his face. Who else would he have when she was gone?

"Call your friends," she said. "You have more work to do."

II

Weeks later, Libra was joined by Kandyce, Vinzant, and Jack on the grassy hill of a cemetery. The sky was clear and the playground Libra and his mother would walk past every day could be seen in the distance across the street. They all stared at the slab of stone with Libra's mother's name on it. It was placed right next to Libra's father's tombstone, and fresh flowers had been placed all around just a moment ago.

Libra was heartbroken, but was surprised it wasn't to the degree he'd expected. He wished she was still around, but was happy his mother didn't have to suffer anymore. He found even more calm when Kandyce and Vinzant hugged him from either side, with Jack's hand on his shoulder. They stayed like that for a moment until Libra took a deep breath and turned to face them all.

"One of the last things my mother told me was that we have more work to do. I don't know about you guys, but I don't want to go back to the past. I don't want this to be the last time we see each other. I want to move forward."

"So, what are you saying?" asked Kandyce.

"Would you consider continuing what we started? I don't want to be the Auctorat by myself anymore. And I couldn't ask for a better group."

To his surprise, they all started smiling and sharing glances with each other. For a second, he felt like he was on the outside of joke.

Vinzant laughed. "Are you kidding? We were just waiting for you to ask."

Libra smiled, and his mourning turned to joy. He felt it in every fiber of his being. It was like his body was getting a calm, slow adrenaline rush. He turned back to his mother's grave and knelt down. "You hear that, Mom? We're gonna go do some work."

When he looked up across the street to the playground, he saw a black-hooded figure turn and disappear further along the path. Libra knew he was being watched the whole time. And he knew who had been watching.

III

Libra entered his warehouse hideout alone. The others would be moving in tomorrow, so he decided he could tidy some things up for them. Something caught his eye on the checkerboard table. It was a brand-new sword and BAC rifle ornately decorated in gold accents. Libra picked them up and marveled over the details. Then, he saw a folded piece of paper. He flipped it open and read the handwritten note:

> *I know these gifts don't make up for my mistakes, but I hope they can be of some help. I'm sorry. May these weapons only be in the hands of those who make history.*
>
> *-Micks*

Despite not saying anything, Libra had already forgiven Micks. He hoped Micks found what he was looking for.

Libra let the weight of the BAC fall on his shoulders as he slipped on the strap. He swung the sword a few times, getting used to its weight, and anticipated the adventures to come.

IV

"Kandyce," called Libra. "A little light could help right about now." He had been busy blocking attacks with his sword, but just barely. He was outside in a dark alley, fending off members of the XN gang who had attempted to get away with the money they took. The way Libra surprised them let him know they hadn't expected to fight anyone, but he didn't want to lose the advantage.

"Just a minute," she called back, fending off attacks of her own.

A shot sounded from her left and the man she'd been fighting collapsed, clutching his leg. "I got him, Kandyce," said Vinzant.

She checked the new large crystal in her pocket. It glowed a bright red, ready for use. "I'm coming," she said. She avoided being knocked over by one of the men that Jack had just tackled. "Watch out guys!" She raised her hand and made it come alight with fire.

Libra smirked, watching it all. He pushed back the guy he'd been fighting and watched him, and the

214

others panic as their jackets began burning, enveloped in flame. This gave them all enough time to knock everyone out and restrain their hands behind their backs. Kandyce removed the fire from each of the gang members and snuffed it out with a closing of her fist.

"Good job, guys," said Libra. "Let's get our bounty."

They each grabbed one of the bound gang members and started walking them away. Only Vinzant paused.

Before moving on with the rest of the group, he pulled out a can of red spray paint and commemorated the moment. They needed a symbol. Something that would let the criminals of Probuston know to tread lightly. He painted a calligraphic 'A' enclosed in a circle.

The Auctorati were in town.

ACKNOWLEDGMENTS

First off, I'd like to thank the fans — those of you who read *Pangaea: Unsettled Land* and pushed me into digging more into this world. This book was made because of you.

I'd like to thank my friends and family for encouraging me and just being there. This was written in a time where I questioned whether I even had another book in me. I doubted if being an author even suited me. Just by being there, you helped me take a breath and keep going.

I'm super grateful to the guidance of my beta readers as well as my editors, Jason Scott and Amelia Beamer. You've all helped me take this to a level that is worthy of showing the world.

To big adventures. To family.

ABOUT THE AUTHOR

Jarrod works in search engine optimization (SEO) and is a graduate of Temple University. When not writing stories or website copy, he enjoys playing tennis or watching a fun TV show with a delicious cup of coffee. He currently lives in Haverford, PA.

And be sure to give *The Auctorati* a review on Amazon, Goodreads, or wherever you can. Let your voice be heard and help this author make more of what you love.

CONTINUE THE STORY

Read *Pangaea: Unsettled Land*, the book that sets up the world of Pangaea in which *The Auctorati* takes place.

When soon-to-be college graduate hears of an ancient mythical sword that's said to have brought magic to the world, he teams up with his best friend and a handsome warrior in search of its secrets. This leads them down a path to confront elemental spirits, magical creatures, a bloodthirsty magic user, and the queen with plans to take power all for herself.

Sign up to get an exciting short story and first notice of future releases by this author.

www.jarrodking.com/subscribe